TH

The adored daughter of Henry VIII, Mary Tudor knew only happiness until she was eleven. Then Henry cast aside Mary's mother, Catherine of Aragon, for his mistress, Anne Boleyn.

Mary was plunged into a nightmare world of brutal guardians and Protestant plots. Inevitably she sought solace in her Catholic faith.

And when she became Queen of England, Mary chose a Spanish bridegroom. Infatuated with Philip of Spain, Mary let him persuade her to stamp out the Protestant faith. The martyrs' fires were kindled and the people named their Queen Bloody Mary.

Remorselessly Mary followed the dictates of her husband – only to have him desert her, leaving her to die a bitter, disillusioned woman.

Also available in this series

VICTORIA by Evelyn Anthony
AN UNKNOWN WELSHMAN by Jean Stubbs
SON OF YORK by Julia Hamilton

Editorial Adviser: Julia Watson

The Spanish Tudor

FREDA M. LONG

A Novel of Mary Tudor

SPHERE BOOKS LIMITED
30/32 Gray's Inn Road, London WC1X 8JL

First published in Great Britain in 1968 by Robert Hale Limited

First Sphere Books edition 1973

Set in Intertype Baskerville

Printed in Great Britain by
Hazell Watson & Viney Ltd
Aylesbury, Bucks

ISBN 0 7221 5595 6

CONTENTS

PRINCIPAL CHARACTERS

Mary Tudor, Princess of Wales, later became Mary I, Queen of England.

Margaret, Countess of Salisbury, niece of King Edward IV and governess to the Princess Mary.

Henry VIII, King of England.

Catherine of Aragon, Henry VIII's first wife and mother to the Princess Mary.

Lady Elizabeth Hammond, lady-in-waiting to Queen Catherine.

The Emperor Charles V, King of Spain and Emperor of Germany.

Cardinal Thomas Wolsey, Archbishop of York and Lord Chancellor.

John Dudley, Chamberlain to the Princess Mary, later Earl of Warwick and Duke of Northumberland.

Peg, a serving-woman at Ludlow Castle.

Jane Dormer
Susan Clarencieux
ladies-in-waiting to the Princess Mary.

Master John Featherstone, tutor to the Princess Mary.

The Lady Anne Boleyn, later to become Henry VIII's second wife and Queen of England.

Princess Elizabeth, daughter of Henry VIII and Queen Anne.

Thomas Cromwell, Principal Secretary to King Henry, later became Master of the Rolls and Lord Privy Seal.

Eustace Chapuys, Spanish Ambassador.

Jane Seymour, lady-in-waiting to Queen Anne, later became Henry VIII's third wife.

Madge Shelton, cousin to Queen Anne.

Lady Shelton, mother to Madge Shelton.

Prince Edward, son of Henry VIII and Queen Jane, later became King Edward VI.

Queen Catherine Parr, sixth and last wife to Henry VIII.

Ambrosius Benson, court painter.

Thomas Seymour, Baron Seymour of Sudeley, brother to Queen Jane.

The Lady Jane Grey, great-niece to King Henry. Became Queen for nine days after the death of Edward VI.

Sir Nicholas Throckmorton, Under-Treasurer to Edward VI.
The Lady Anne of Cleves, fourth wife to King Henry—marriage annulled.
Stephen Gardiner, Bishop of Winchester.
Simon Renard, Spanish Ambassador.
Philip of Spain, son and heir to the Emperor Charles V, became the husband of Queen Mary.
Ruy Gomez, principal gentleman to Philip of Spain.
Mistress Blanche Boxley, court midwife.

PART ONE

"Pray Christ save father and mother,
And this young ladye fair,
And send her shortly a brother,
To be England's rightful heir."

16th Century Poem. Anon.

RICHMOND PALACE

July, 1557

She sat, a small, spare woman, past the prime of life, peering out through the dust-blurred windows of her presence chamber. Her sight was very poor now and the grey eyes saw little of the garden beyond the windows where the bachelors' buttons, heartsease and snapdragons bloomed with extravagant prodigality in the knot garden. The cockle-shell mount, adorned by stone heraldic beasts holding rods, upon which gilded vanes turned idly in the light breeze, could be dimly discerned by those same grey eyes which had seen more than their fair share of this world's sorrows. The short, thick, heavily be-ringed hands fluttered in the black velvet lap, and one reached up to touch the greying red hair beneath her hood. Her strong housewifely instincts told her that Richmond was long overdue for cleansing and that it was time the court moved on to another palace, but a certain apathy had descended upon her of late, strangling her will-power and sapping her energy. The days were long and lonely with her lord gone out of England. No child stirred in her womb, and it seemed to her that God, who had been her consolation since childhood, had turned His face from her. Only fear swelled and burgeoned under her heart, mocking her in the cold, dark watches of the night when sleep eluded her. Then would a small insistent voice, dredged up from the depths of her soul, call her traitor and tell her that she had betrayed England into the hands of Spain. The voice of her conscience was a hard thing to live with, but live with it she must. She thought it a small price to pay for her sinful folly.

"Oh Mother of Mercy," she prayed, plucking at the soft folds of her gown, "why did'st Thou see fit to deny me the blessing of a child?" What joy had been hers, after her marriage to Philip, when she thought herself to be with child, and how happy did she and her ladies busy themselves with preparations for its coming. The cradle had been made of good Welsh oak, fashioned lovingly for her by Welsh craftsmen, whom she liked to think remembered her with affection from the old days when she had sojourned at Ludlow Castle. The carving was exquisite. Fleur-de-lys and Tudor roses abounded; lions of England romped with Welsh dragons all round the sides, and there was a Latin inscription on the hood, *God Keep This Child*. How touched she had been when she saw that those work-scarred hands had not been able to resist carving underneath the Welsh translation of the inscription as though to remind her that the child, if a boy, would be their prince. Such a beautiful cradle. It lay now at Hampton Court in some forgotten chamber, along with all the other items which were never needed. She neither knew nor cared where. After her bitter disappointment she had bidden her dear friend Jane Dormer have everything put away so that she would no longer have to look upon those sad reminders of a precious hope unfulfilled. Jane had done her work well, but not well enough, for only that day she had come across the set of baby clothes made for her by her sister Elizabeth. She had found them in the chest where she kept her hoods. She had taken them out and tried to summon a laugh at Elizabeth's lack of skill as a needlewoman, but as she gazed on the lop-sided coronets decorating each jacket and smock, a terrible wave of grief overcame her and the quick, hot tears coursed down her cheeks until her eyelids grew puffy and her head ached unbearably. Elizabeth. Mark Smeaton's brat! Ah, no, Mary, you know that is not true, but you would like to have it so because you cannot bear to think of Anne Boleyn's daughter wearing your crown.

She pressed trembling finger-tips to her throbbing temples. Oh God, how her head ached. Why was she raking over all these dead ashes? She did not know. She knew only that her unhappiness must find some expression. She must try to re-live the events in her crowded life just as they had happened. Find out where she had gone wrong and purge her soul. Perhaps then she could die with a quiet mind. Perhaps . . .

GREENWICH PALACE

June, 1522

I

Her mind went back to a hot June night in the year 1522. She was six years old. The Princess Mary of England, heiress-presumptive to the throne. Her ladies were putting her to bed in her chamber at Greenwich Palace and their talk was all of the ceremony which was to take place on the morrow. Then was the princess to be formally betrothed to the Emperor Charles V of Spain. Outside, beyond the windows with their patterned lead cames, the birds trilled forth their vesper songs, producing sweet harmonies of sound to lull her to sleep. If she listened carefully Mary could hear the tinkling splash of the fountain playing perpetually in the walled garden. She could not take her eyes off the gown, hanging on its wooden frame, which she would wear to be presented to her betrothed. It was of violet velvet with an undergown of frosted silver, and to go with it there was a pair of false sleeves, slashed and puffed in the new style and embroidered with double-headed eagles in black silk, a pretty compliment to the Emperor. How vain a child she was. How she loved fine clothes and jewels.

Margaret, Countess of Salisbury, Mary's kinswoman and governess, divested her of the last article of clothing, a white lawn chemise, and with a "There child, up with you!" hoisted her into the enormous bed which would have comfortably accommodated eight children of her size. Mary shivered ecstatically as the cool sheets caressed her naked body. She slid down into the bed until the covers reached her chin. Suddenly she emerged, to sit bolt upright.

"Aunt!" she called, on a high, childish treble, "my night-rail if you please. The Queen is coming to bid me good night."

This was a special event for Mary as her mother, formerly a princess of Spain, followed the custom of the Spanish court and was wont to bid her daughter a formal good night in the hall after supper.

The countess regarded her charge laughingly with her shrewd, kindly brown eyes and Mary marvelled, not for the first time, at how like she was to the portraits of her own great-grandfather, Edward the Fourth, two of which hung in the great hall at Greenwich. He was the countess's uncle, she being the daughter of George, Duke of Clarence, his brother. The countess had Edward's face with its long, straight nose and wide-lipped mouth. Only her eyes were different, being brown instead of blue.

"God-a-mercy child," she said now, "and has your mother never seen you in naked bed ere this? Why so prim?"

"Tomorrow I am to be betrothed," answered Mary with dignity, as though this explained everything.

The Duchess of Norfolk who was putting away Mary's pearl head-tire in the jewel coffer, laughed over her shoulder at the child. She was a small, fussy woman with bright, black eyes and a tiny, almost non-existent snub-nose. "Would your grace prefer the black lace or the scarlet flurt silk?" she asked teasingly.

Mary blushed at this raillery and all the ladies smiled, gathering about her bed to kiss and hug her. They spoiled her shamelessly and would not have her teased. A night-rail was quickly produced and placed about the thin white shoulders. Mistress Alice Baker, one of her bedchamber women, was brushing Mary's hair when the child's quick ear caught the sound of approaching footsteps.

"Mother!" she exclaimed eagerly, her eyes glued to the door.

Catherine of Aragon, Queen of England, came through the door on silent feet the while her daughter watched, fascinated, this being whom she loved best in the whole world. At this time Catherine was thirty-seven years old. She was short of stature and inclined now to stoutness, though she had been slender enough in her youth. Her face was pale-complexioned. Grey-green eyes looked calmly out at the world above a blunt nose and a small, delicately-shaped mouth. Her hair, a pale sandy yellow, was almost totally concealed beneath her gable hood. She was not a beautiful woman, but she had a kind of dignified serenity which transcended beauty. To Mary's adoring eyes she was all that was perfect. To those less biased, Catherine's rigid upbringing at the court of Spain made her oft-times appear coldly aloof and unbending.

With surprising grace for so heavy a woman, she moved towards the bed and took Mary's outstretched hands in her own, squeezing them gently. The thick white fingers moved to stroke her daughter's newly burnished hair, pushing it back from the hot, radiant little face. Her perfume, an unusual distillation compounded of essence of rosemary and cinnamon, hung on the air.

"You are flushed sweetheart," she admonished, in the high, fluting voice which had such amazing carrying power. "I told you, did I not, that to get over-excited is unbecoming in a princess. You must try to remain calm."

"Yes, Mother."

"Well-a-day," Catherine said indulgently, her mouth curving into one of her rare, sweet smiles, "perhaps it is only to be expected. You are to be betrothed to a very great prince indeed, my daughter."

"Your nephew, Mother," said Mary dimpling, as though Catherine needed to be reminded of this very pleasing fact.

The Queen's smile broadened. "Yes, sweetheart, my nephew. I confess it gives me great satisfaction that you should have a Spanish bridegroom. It has been my constant prayer that it would be so."

"How fortunate, Mother," replied the child, "that my betrothal to the Dauphin of France was broken."

Catherine's smile disappeared, to be replaced by a slight frown. "You do not remember that, my daughter. You were but two years old at the time the betrothal was made."

"Oh no, I do not remember, Mother," answered Mary brightly, "but my lady of Norfolk told me all about it, and about the banquet when my lord of Norfolk drank too much wine and fell under the table."

The duchess, who could not fail to overhear the conversation between mother and daughter, tried hard to look unconcerned. Catherine regarded her friend with some severity. She was disturbed by the reminder of an alliance with France, a country whose King she detested.

Mary, as though conscious that her words were ill-timed, and indeed she did sense her mother's displeasure, said contritely, "I have offended you, Mother?"

At once the severe lines of Catherine's face softened again. "No, no, sweetheart, you have not offended me." She continued briskly, "Now, my daughter, you have remembered all that you must do on the morrow?"

"Yes, Mother."

"Repeat it for me."

Catherine signed to her ladies to bring her a stool and when it was placed beside the bed she sat down and ran a finger round the edge of her gable hood, easing it back on her head. The striped silk sheaths which crossed over under the gable point had left an angry mark on her forehead, and some of her sandy hair was thus exposed. Now she looked younger, more vulnerable somehow. She folded her hands in her lap, after smoothing the skirt of her sober grey gown, and gazed at her daughter expectantly.

Mary straightened her back and frowned importantly. She coughed delicately and unnecessarily to preface her words and noted with satisfaction that nearly every eye in the chamber was fixed upon her. What a spoiled child she was.

"When I enter the great hall," she began, "I am to walk slowly towards the dais whereon you will be seated with Father and the Emperor. I must first make my obeisance to the Emperor, as he is our guest, and then must I curtsy to Your Majesties. I am then to take my place on the cushion provided for me at father's feet."

Catherine nodded approvingly and Mary continued. "Cardinal Wolsey will read the marriage treaty and then Father and the Emperor will sign it. After the signing the Emperor will place the betrothal ring on my finger." She sighed with childish exaggeration. "And then I suppose we shall all have to listen to a sermon from the Cardinal."

Suppressed giggles filled the chamber and even Catherine covered her mouth with her hand to conceal the beginnings of a smile.

"And listen to it you shall, you impudent child," she rebuked. "The Cardinal will discourse on the dignity and honourableness of the married state and you will do well to mark his every word."

Her own words held no sting, however, and Mary leaned towards her to say with some anxiety, "Is the Emperor Charles handsome, Mother?"

"As to that, you must wait and see," replied Catherine with a hint of mischief. "And now my daughter I shall bid you good night, but first you shall see the gifts I have brought for you to wear on the morrow."

Mary expelled her breath on a windy sigh of relief and her mother looked at her reproachfully. "You did not think I had forgot?"

"No, Mother!" lied Mary joyfully.

Catherine called to the Lady Elizabeth Hammond, one of her gentlewomen, who, at her command, approached Mary's bed. Being somewhat short of sight the child had not noticed that Lady Hammond was holding two objects in her hands. As she advanced Mary's eye was attracted by the larger object and she could scarce speak, so great was her pleasure. "A hood!" she exclaimed. "A French hood!"

Lady Hammond held up the hood and all the ladies gathered round to admire it. It was made in the new French fashion and did not resemble the English gable hood in the smallest degree. Instead of the ugly pointed arch, so unflattering to female faces, this one curved softly to frame the head and show more of the hair. It was fashioned in violet velvet stiffened with buckram canvas and with a nether billement of goldsmith's work. The upper billement was decorated with pearls.

So animated did the ladies become over the hood that Catherine was forced to command them to silence, though not very severely. The other gift pleased Mary just as much for it was a miniature of her mother and father set in a diamond-studded frame and suspended from a fine gold chain. She would wear it on her girdle. Impulsively, the child stretched forth her arms and for once Catherine allowed herself to be hugged and wetly kissed. When Mary released her mother she saw that there were tears in her eyes. Hastily the Queen brushed them away, rose, and gently pushed Mary back upon her pillows. *"Buenas noches, querida,"* she murmured, and was gliding away when Mary, struck by a thought, called urgently after her, "Mother! I shall not have to go and live in Spain shall I?"

Catherine turned and her expression startled Mary. Such an intensity of pain marred the calm features. "No, my child, not for a long, long time yet. Not till you are grown to womanhood." Catherine trembled slightly. Mary's question had terrified her.

"And then shall I go, and shall I have children? Will the Holy Spirit bring them?"

The Duchess of Norfolk gave a snort of unseemly laughter and Mary saw Catherine redden. "You will have children if God wills it," she said and only Mary missed the wistful note in her voice. She added, "You must sleep now, my daughter, else shall I be very much displeased with you."

Catherine spoke more sharply than she had intended and frowned at my lady of Norfolk who, irrepressible as ever, shrugged and pursed her lips. The Queen was always reproving the duchess for some breach of etiquette, but there was, none the less, a very strong bond of affection between them.

2

Catherine was gone and Mary lay. dreamily counting the Tudor roses and Beaufort portcullises embroidered in gold thread on her crimson bed hangings, and listening contentedly to the chatter of her ladies which grew fainter and fainter as she drifted into sleep.

She was on the edge of oblivion when the sound of footsteps and the baying of deep, masculine voices, forced her back into wakefulness. The door fairly burst open and to her intense delight her father erupted into the chamber followed by at least eight of his gentlemen. Tut-tutting loudly the Countess of Salisbury sketched the King a very inelegant curtsy and said, as though speaking to a badly behaved child, "Not the gentlemen, too, Sire. The princess will be fit for naught on the morrow. She is overly excited as it is."

So saying, the countess made shooing motions at Henry's brilliantly attired gentlemen who backed away hurriedly like a gaggle of startled geese.

Good-humouredly Henry VIII, King of England, bowed to her wishes and signed to his gentlemen to quit the chamber. Handsome Charles Brandon, Duke of Suffolk, married to Aunt Mary Tudor, managed to evade the countess's flapping arms, and came to the foot of Mary's bed. He winked broadly at her before being hustled away with the others. Though but six years old Mary blushed furiously and was glad that her ladies had forgotten to remove her night-rail which she clutched instinctively to her flat chest.

Henry plumped himself down on the bed, a huge, glittering figure in emerald and gold brocade. Mary's ladies, having recovered from their surprise at his coming, were busying themselves by lighting the candles in their tall metal sconces, although it was not yet quite dark. Mary noticed with customary pleasure the way her father's finger rings sparkled and flared in the soft golden light. Henry regarded her teasingly, his grey eyes twinkling. His short, thick fingers pulled at his neatly-trimmed tawny beard and he waggled his tongue at her between small red lips. She squealed with delight and bounced up and down on her feather mattress. Deeply though she loved her mother she knew, with a child's swift, sure instinct, that Catherine would never countenance what she called light behaviour, whereas father, dearest father, was complacent to a degree.

"So we are to be betrothed to *el Emperador* no less," Henry said roguishly. "Soon we shall be too proud to speak to our poor old father who is only a King." He dabbed at mock tears on his cheek.

Mary giggled. "Oh, Father!"

"A handsome Emperor, too," Henry elaborated slyly.

"Is he so?" she breathed.

"He is indeed and lusty too by the looks of him."

"Lusty?" she queried innocently.

Henry caught the countess's disapproving eye upon him and said hastily, "Er . . . strong and brave."

At this point Mary's vanity overcame her decorum and she asked with shameful coyness, "And shall I make a pretty Empress, Father?"

Henry's loud laugh rang out, filling the chamber with reverberating sound. He reached into his huge slashed sleeve and produced a hand-mirror set in a frame of solid gold. He held it out to her. "It seems I chose well when I purchased your betrothal gift," he said. "Your uncle of Suffolk said you would like better a necklace, but methinks he was wrong. Now you can see for yourself how pretty an Empress you will make."

"For me?" she asked incredulously, stretching out her hand for the mirror. She experienced a momentary sense of guilt. Mother surely could not have approved of such a gift, pandering as it did to her vanity.

"For you, sweetheart," Henry confirmed.

Embarrassed now by her boldness Mary glanced briefly at her reflection in the mirror and then laid the shimmering object, glass side down, on the bed-cover. Her father was smiling at her benevolently and she was further emboldened to ask, "Father, if God sends me a son when I am married, he will be King of England one day will he not?"

The words had barely left her mouth before the child became aware that she had made a terrible mistake. She heard a swift intake of breath from some of her ladies and when she looked at her father's face she was filled with fear. It was no longer smiling. The widely arched, sandy brows were knit close together and the small, womanish lips were drawn back over the strong white teeth. "Who told you that?" he rasped. The tone of his voice made her tremble.

"Th . . . th . . . the D . . . D . . . Duchess of Norfolk," she stammered, and then, to make matters infinitely worse, "My lady of Norfolk says mother will have no more babies."

"Does she so?" Henry rose, shot the duchess a glance of pure venom and snapped, "Thy fat tongue is too big for thy mouth, Elizabeth Tilney."

He left abruptly. As the chamber door slammed behind him the Countess of Salisbury rounded on the duchess and rated her soundly for her indiscretion. Poor duchess. It was a considerable feat, even for her, to displease both King and Queen in the space of a single day.

Forcing back the insistent tears which Catherine had told her were so undignified in a high-born lady, Mary watched miserably while the countess and the duchess wrangled. Later, when all save the lady on duty had retired from her chamber, she lay, wakeful and deflated, gazing up at the painted ceiling, counting the abandoned, naked cherubs above her head. She heard the court usher calling, "Have in for all night good sirs! Have in!" which meant that all those who had Bouche of Court were being summoned for the last meal of the day. It also meant that the King was now in bed, naked as the sword which lay within easy reach of his right hand. Oh, sweet Virgin, prayed the child, make him forgive me for whatever it is I have said to offend him.

3

The betrothal day itself stood out like a beacon in her memory. It was one of the few days in her life when she remembered being truly happy, though God knew she had been, up till then, a spoiled and pampered child. But the time was fast approaching when she would no longer continue to be so.

Her ladies brought her into the great hall of Greenwich Palace at ten o'clock in the morning. All the court was assembled there and Henry and Catherine, together with the Emperor, were already seated on the dais. Cardinal Wolsey hovered, not too unobtrusively, behind them.

Mary felt very self-conscious in her new gown and hood and the hot blood suffused her cheeks as every eye in the hall was turned upon her. The painted glass of the windows which depicted the royal arms and badges seemed to rush by her in a dizzy riot of colour and indeed she had begun to walk too fast for she felt a restraining hand on her arm and looked up at the countess who, with a slight shake of her head, slowed her down to a mere crawl. Wildly her eyes sought the gilded spandrels and carved pendants above her head, and the great blue louvre dotted with silver and gold stars which formed the focal point of the ornate ceiling. Blue and gold, crimson and green. The colours made her head spin and she swayed on her feet. Though she loved bright colours she could not gaze on them for any length of time without feeling the onset of a migraine. She forced herself to look straight in front of her. She was almost at the dais now and her father and mother were sitting there, both smiling broadly at her. Mary offered up a prayer of thanksgiving to the Virgin for She had obviously interceded for her and put the King in a good humour. Thanks, Holy Mother, she breathed. He is no longer displeased with me.

So far she had not dared to raise her eyes to the Emperor's face but now, as she accorded him a well practised, deep curtsy she was surprised to find long-fingered hands lifting her to her feet. Shyly she looked up into the bluest eyes she had ever seen. They smiled down at her above the crooked nose and large fleshy mouth. The chin, out-thrust like all the Habsburgs, was partly obscured by a short, raven-black beard. His hair matched his beard and was topped by a black velvet cap decorated with a sapphire which Mary judged to be as big as her father's thumb-nail. The prognathous jaw loomed towards her and before she knew it Charles had kissed her on both cheeks, calling forth a murmur of sentimental approval from the assembled company. So disconcerted was she by this charming, unexpected gesture that her cheeks became even redder if that were possible and she completely forgot to make her devoirs to her mother and father. Charles's black and silver-clad figure was still bending over her and then, to her consternation, for surely the marriage-treaty should have been signed first, he had encircled her thumb with a ring set with a step-cut emerald the size of a walnut. "I think your other fingers be too small, princess," he said. "Your thumb will have to serve until you be grown a little more." He spoke well-nigh perfect English with the merest trace of accent. Tongue-tied she gawped up at him while the ladies emitted, "Oohs" and "Aahs" of astonishment at the size of the jewel winking on her thumb.

At this point Cardinal Wolsey stepped forward from behind Catherine's chair of state and coughed importantly. He had noticed the Emperor's mistake if others had not. From beneath his scarlet robe he produced the all-important marriage treaty and signed to his Secretary, George Cavendish, a tall, thin, spear of a man, to bring pens, ink and wax for the sealing. Wolsey the omniscient, ever-watchful of his royal master's interests, the Ipswich butcher's son who had risen far above his humble beginnings to become Archbishop of York, a Cardinal, Lord Chancellor and Papal Legate. Mary could not remember a time when his presence had not loomed large in her young life. His red-clad figure plodding ponderously about the court was a familiar sight, the huge head swaying from side to side, the small, protruding yellow eyes, deep-set in the fleshy, red-nosed face, searching, searching, his mind busy with affairs of state and his complicated foreign policy.

The treaty was duly signed and sealed and Wolsey, tucking plump, be-ringed hands into costly caffa sleeves, advanced to within a few feet of where Mary sat on her purple cushion and prepared to deliver his carefully prepared homily on the married state, of which he was supposed to know nothing. But the Cardinal, as many there knew, had his secrets. Mary braced herself and looked up at him dutifully. She put up a hand to her beautiful hood, feeling unnecessarily to see if it was still in place. Catherine, who was seated behind and a little to one side of her, gently removed the offending hand and returned it to her daughter's lap.

Wolsey coughed again, opened his mouth and began. "Your Imp . . ." His words died on a sort of choked splutter as Henry declaimed in a loud voice, "Enough, my lord Cardinal. We shall dispense with oratory. The Emperor did not come here to listen to you sermonise and my daughter is but six. She has not yet sufficient years to understand your homily and little enough inclination to listen to it I'll warrant."

Wolsey's ruddy-toned face deepened to an unhealthy blotched purple. The King's interruption was unprecedented. He might have had the good taste to warn him beforehand. As it was he, Cardinal Wolsey, had been made to look a complete fool.

Mary, meanwhile, stuffed her fist into her mouth to stifle a disrespectful giggle. Behind her she heard Catherine protesting. "Your Grace, since the Cardinal worked far into the night preparing . . ."

"His work shall not be wasted," Henry broke in jovially, if a trifle rudely. "He can save it until Mary be of proper age."

"Perhaps, my lord Cardinal," said Catherine primly, "you

will have Cavendish copy out the sermon in English. Then the princess may translate it into the Latin when she is at her studies."

Wolsey inclined his head and smiled palely at Catherine. Mary's heart sank but lifted again as Henry roared, "No, no, that she shall not, poor lass. 'Twill addle her brains. I say it shall be left until later and there's an end to the matter."

Catherine lapsed into hurt silence, Wolsey looked discomfited and the Emperor tried to keep a straight face. This was probably the first time that the King had publicly rebuked either the Queen or the Cardinal and there were many present on that day who were later convinced that this had been a sign of the dreadful change which was soon to take place in him.

The rest of that day had a dream-like quality for Mary. She dimly recalled in later years that Henry whisked the Emperor off on a hunting expedition and that the party returned half an hour after the appointed time for the betrothal banquet. The Queen became extremely agitated and fell to wringing her hands with little futile gestures.

The banquet was a splendid affair. Mary could not resist peeping into the hall to watch the elaborate preparations for it. Carvers, sewerers. ewerers and sundry other household officers rushed about in all directions under the sharp eye of the Steward, whose voice rose to a strident scream when something was not ordered to his liking. Musicians crowded into the gallery and soon the unmelodious sound of lutes, rebecks and guitars being tuned rent the air. Mary was particularly fascinated by the assaying of the salt, an ancient piece of ceremonial which necessitated the Taster probing the salt in four different places with a wedge of bread which he passed on to the Panter to eat. As always Mary held her breath then heaved a sigh of relief as the Panter ate the bread, remained mercifully unaffected and the Taster bawled, "Salt unsullied, my lord Steward!"

At the banquet Mary was the focus of attention. She sat between her mother and the Emperor at the high table on the dais and everyone complimented her on her appearance until she fell to blushing again and Catherine began to frown, a sure sign of disapproval. Henry ignored his wife's frowns and reaching across to where Mary sat proudly beside her betrothed, he tore off her hood so that her red-gold hair tumbled about her shoulders. "There, highness!" he roared.

"Do you not think 'tis a fair bargain you have made?" He was more than a little drunk.

Mary looked up at Charles uncertainly. He was smiling, but the smile was a little strained. "A fair bargain indeed," he commented, "but I should be better pleased if Your Majesties would allow the princess to come to the court of Spain so that she may be schooled for her future role as Queen and Empress."

Mary felt little shivers rippling down her spine. She heard Catherine give a little gasp and whisper an involuntary "No!"

Henry's boisterous joviality subsided a little as he said gruffly, "No need for that, highness. The child already speaks Spanish passing fair and she shall be brought up in all respects like a Spanish lady. The Queen has not forgot her own upbringing. She will school our daughter." His manner became genial again. "Why, she shall even wear Spanish dress if it pleases you." He looked expectantly at Charles.

Charles nodded gravely as if giving this point serious consideration, then said almost casually, "She will one day be my Empress. It is essential that she shall be fitted for the important task that lies ahead of her. However, she will also be Queen of this realm in her own right and I sympathise with your natural desire to keep her here."

The silence was so thick that it could have been cleft in two. Henry's voice was ice-cold as he demanded, "Does the Emperor mean to suggest that I shall not father a male heir for England?" His breathing, rasping and heavy, filled the uneasy silence.

For the first time in her life Mary saw an expression of pure fright cross her mother's face. Charles, however, remained coolly unperturbed. He said easily, "I am but stating the position as it stands at present. Doubtless God in His infinite wisdom and mercy will send Your Majesties a son in due time. I pray that it may be so."

"The devil he does!" murmured Charles Brandon to the Earl of Arundel.

Henry's brows were set in a fierce scowl. Muttering to himself he attacked his food. Swiftly Catherine signalled to the musicians to strike up and within half an hour a more relaxed atmosphere had been restored. Mary nodded over her glazed apples and the Emperor smiled his enigmatic smile.

LUDLOW CASTLE

August, 1525–July, 1527

I

Margaret, Countess of Salisbury, jounced along uncomfortably on the skittish little roan mare which had replaced her own fat, easy-gaited gelding. A few appropriately vehement masculine oaths sprang to her lips as she cursed the ill-luck which had caused Balthazar to cast a shoe a mile or two back. She'd wager the nearest smithy was at least ten miles farther along the road. August! What a month to be travelling from London to Wales and in calvalcade too, with the ruts in the road baked hard as iron.

The air was moist and heavy and a myriad small insects hovered about the countess's sweat-streaked face. Savagely she slashed at them with her riding whip and they dispersed in a buzzing cloud. She began to wonder why they were going to Wales at all. It seemed almost like banishment. That was nonsense, of course. The King had seen fit to confer on his only daughter the title of Princess of Wales, a signal and unusual honour, and had decided that she should preside at the head of her own household at Ludlow Castle. The Queen, on hearing of the King's decision, had voiced a feeble protest, but she had been quickly frowned to silence by a new, strangely intolerant Henry, who had brusquely ordered her to, "Hold your peace, lady!" Catherine had consoled herself with the thought that her very dear friend and kinswoman by marriage, the Countess of Salisbury, would be going with her beloved daughter to Ludlow, a place which held bitter, secret memories for her. Behind the grey stone walls of Ludlow Castle had been enacted the brief tragedy of her first marriage to Arthur, Prince of Wales, elder brother to King Henry. There had she watched the thin, slightly malformed youth, of whom she had grown quite fond, cough his life away, a victim of the sweating sickness. No, Catherine did not like Ludlow and she shuddered when she thought that her daughter would be entombed within those same grey walls.

After bidding Mary a gravely calm farewell, which masked the turmoil within her breast, Catherine had taken the countess to one side and urged her to see that Mary took plenty of exercise in the intervals between her studies. "Take her out of the castle whenever possible," she had said, and there had been a beseeching note in her voice, completely foreign to her. "Promise me, Margaret," she had begged. Understanding, mixed with pity, had gleamed in the countess's sharp brown eyes and she had placed her hand gently on Catherine's arm as she said, "I promise, Madam. The child shall walk or ride whenever the weather be clement." Catherine's answering smile had almost slipped out of place as she bade the countess God-speed.

The dust swirled and eddied about the roan's hooves and the countess dabbed at her red-rimmed eyes with a kerchief. Blessed Virgin but she was too old for this sort of thing. Why, she had been fifty-two at Easter, an age when most women of her station in life had retired to their country manors to live out the rest of their days in peaceful contemplation of their beehives and herb gardens. She thought about the chantry chapel in Christchurch Priory waiting to receive her soulless body. Built of specially imported Caen stone by English and Italian craftsmen, its foliated arches with their richly carved finials were a wonder to behold, the whole a delicately modelled miniature church. Ah well, she'd had a good life, despite the dynastic troubles which had surrounded all the Plantagenets after the Tudor accession, and the loss of a very dear brother, the Earl of Warwick, who had been sacrificed to the Tudor ambition. It was fortunate for the countess that she could not see into the future to a day when she herself would stand on the scaffold on Tower Green, a sacrifice to the Tudor tyranny.

The small cavalcade, some fifty souls in all, comprising all the members of the Princess Mary's newly-established household, wound its way slowly onwards through the sun-scorched countryside of Worcestershire. The scenery was breathtaking. Purple-capped hills rolled away into the distance, their peaks nudging the hot blue sky, and in the green valleys gay little rivulets chattered and bubbled their way over sandstone beds to the sea.

The countess looked down at the diminutive figure of the Princess Mary, now in her tenth year, riding beside her on a white jennet, given to her as a betrothal gift by the Emperor Charles. The child, trim and neat in a green velvet riding habit, was unaccountably silent and her usually pink complexion had paled to a creamy white. The countess hoped devoutly that Mary was not sickening. The physicians were two days behind them, the King having had some trouble in their selection. Henry was selfish where his physicians were concerned. Somewhat of a hypochondriac, he liked to keep the best for himself. Maybe, thought the countess, the child was just moping over the defection of her betrothed who had very ungallantly declared his intention of marrying the Princess Isabel of Portugal. The countess clucked her tongue impatiently. It was all the fault of the princess's younger ladies. Such nonsense they had filled her head with, telling her that the Emperor was dying of love for her and persuading her that she was dying of love for him. That brat Margaret Douglas had been responsible for much of the damage. The daughter of the King's eldest sister, Margaret Tudor, by her second marriage to Archibald Douglas, Earl of Angus, the Douglas child was the same age as her cousin Mary and she had her mother's wild predilection for the opposite sex. Margaret Tudor had been married to King James IV of Scotland until he fell at the battle of Flodden Field. She had allowed less than a year to pass before marrying the Earl of Angus. Her black-haired chit of a daughter was riding behind them now making cow eyes at the squires. She'd find herself in serious trouble one of these days. The countess pursued her gloomy train of thought. Wolsey had not helped. Forcing the child to write to the Emperor, and such a letter too, declaring her passion for him and enclosing the emerald ring Charles had given her, an emerald being the symbol of constancy. A neat touch that and typical of Wolsey.

These musings were interrupted by the clatter of hoofbeats and the voice of John Dudley, the princess's Chamberlain. "With your permission, countess, I think a stop for the night at Pershore Abbey yonder would be advisable."

His stubby forefinger indicated the soaring spires of the Abbey church about three miles ahead. " 'Tis past five of the clock and I misdoubt me if there be any suitable accommodation for another twenty miles or more."

The countess nodded emphatically. The sooner she parted company from the roan the better she would like it. "Yes, John, a good idea. God grant the worthy brothers have their own smithy."

"Sure to," said John Dudley, grinning as the countess's

mare skittered forward and nearly unseated her. He was still grinning as he put out a hand to catch the mare's bridle and steady her. The countess looked into the saucy blue eyes and snorted. "Take that smirk off thy face John Dudley and go tell everyone we are stopping for the night," she snapped. Instantly Dudley's face sobered respectfully and he turned his horse smartly about to do the countess's bidding. She watched his departing back. Knows his place, she thought, but an ambitious young man for all that and too fat by far for his age.

Quite suddenly, taking her by surprise, Mary's voice piped up, "Aunt, is not Ludlow Castle the place where mother came when she was wed to my uncle, Prince Arthur?"

Startled by this unexpected question, for she had never known Mary to refer to her mother's previous marriage, the countess managed to say equably enough. "Aye, God assoil him."

"Was mother married to him for long?"

"She was not married to him at all," replied the countess firmly. "His Holiness Pope Julius the Second annulled the marriage after Prince Arthur's death so that it was no marriage at all."

"Does every lady have her marriage annulled if her husband dies before her? When the Earl of Salisbury died was your marriage annulled, aunt?"

The countess felt small beads of perspiration start on her forehead and put up a hand to wipe them away. How could she tell this innocent child that Catherine and Arthur had not slept together in naked bed and that therefore the Pope had seen fit to declare the marriage void, having first obtained a signed statement from two matrons to the effect that Catherine was still *virgo intacta*? She coughed to gain time then said, she hoped convincingly, "Well, no, child, but your mother's case was rather special. She and the prince were but children when they were wed and not considered of proper age."

She had stretched a point here, for both Catherine and Arthur had been fifteen years old when they were married and considered of sufficient years to effect a consummation. The fact that they had not done so could only be attributed to Arthur's delicate disposition and subsequent ill-health.

To her intense relief Mary did not pursue the matter, but

her next question was almost as disconcerting. "Why did the Emperor Charles break our betrothal?"

Jesu, I wish I knew, thought the countess. She dismissed as idle gossip the rumour which had been circulating the court in London for some time to the effect that Henry was thinking of divorcing Catherine because she could not give him a male heir and that Charles had got wind of this. There were some who said that Henry's sole purpose in bestowing the title of Princess of Wales upon his daughter was to give the lie to this rumour. Of course, the notion was utterly ridiculous and just what you would expect from clacking tongues at court. Aloud she said, "The Emperor did not really want to break his betrothal to you, child, but unfortunately for him he had made a pre-contract with the Princess of Portugal and I fear the lady is holding him to his promise."

"Oh." Mary's voice was bleak.

In desperation the countess said, "Perhaps the Emperor was a little too old for you anyway, child."

"Perhaps," replied Mary apathetically.

Suddenly, the countess grew bold and broached a matter which had been on her mind for some time. "How would you like to marry an English gentleman?"

Mary hesitated. "I . . . I . . . I do not know. Mother always said she wanted a Spanish bridegroom for me. It is her constant prayer. Anyway I cannot think of any English gentleman who is high-born enough to ask Father for my hand." This was said without any assumption of pride. Mary was simply stating what she considered to be a fact.

"There is my son Reginald." The countess knew that the Queen would favour such a match for she had said as much. Catherine's conscience had never become reconciled to the fact that her father and mother, Ferdinand and Isabella of Spain, had insisted that the Earl of Warwick, the countess's brother, and the last male Plantagenet then living, should be executed before they would allow their daughter to be married to Prince Arthur.

"Reginald?" queried Mary vaguely. "Why yes, he is of royal blood. I had not thought of him."

"Do you like him?"

"Oh yes, indeed I do. He is very kind and often helps me with my Latin lessons."

"Would it please you if the King and Queen should approve a match with him?"

"He is the same age as the Emperor," Mary pointed out

a trifle desolately. "If the Emperor is too old for me, so is Reginald." And then, as she saw the look of near-dismay on the face of the countess she remembered her manners and added, "But if Father and Mother decide that Reginald shall be my husband I shall be well content."

"Dearest child." Ashamed, the countess placed her arm about Mary's shoulders. How sad it was, all this match-making above the child's head, without a thought for her feelings. She of all people should have known better than to interfere in such a matter. The victim of an arranged marriage herself, she knew only too well what grief such a union could bring. Her brow wrinkled worriedly as she thought about Reginald. He was not happy at court. All the time he felt surrounded by the King's hostility. He was so close to the throne. A male Plantagenet. A marriage to Mary might be the answer for him since it would remove the need for the King's suspicions. But no, it would never be. Reginald had hinted to her before she left London that he might soon find some excuse to leave the court and retire abroad. Take Holy orders perhaps. Sensible. The countess bit her lip and sighed. It would have been nice if he and Mary could have married.

2

Mary and her household arrived at Ludlow Castle on 26 August, 1525. The princess was feeling depressed and out of sorts. It was all very well for her father to make her Princess of Wales, an odd title at best, it usually being reserved for heirs male, but why send her away from the court? She did not want to set up her own household. She would have been quite content to remain at court in London, but father had insisted that now she was Princess of Wales she must govern her principality, and so here she was with her household, separated from the ones she loved most, her father and mother. She could feel the beginnings of a headache and one of her back teeth throbbed dully. Her women were running about like distracted hens, trying to adjust themselves to their new surroundings. Mary waited until she was sure that not a single eye was upon her and set out on a private tour of inspection of the castle.

The first thing she had noticed on arrival was that it smelt musty and uninhabited. The countess had noticed it too, and had given orders for all the doors and windows to be left open so that what air there was could circulate around the dust-filled chambers. The small castle garrison consisted of a handful of elderly servants left over from Prince Arthur's day. Bewildered by this sudden influx of humanity into their peaceful domain, they stood about in silent, unhelpful attitudes.

Mary made her way to the second floor of the castle and traversed the long, damp passages on silent feet. There was nothing much to interest her until, turning a corner, she was suddenly confronted by a portrait of her uncle, Prince Arthur. It hung on a rusty nail beside an oak, brass-studded door. Mary examined it critically. Its replica hung at Greenwich Palace, but this, the original, seemed different somehow, more alive. Green eyes gazed down at her from a long, thin face and the full heavy mouth smiled lazily. He was not a bit like father. Neither was he like the portraits she had seen of her grandmother, Elizabeth of York. There was something of grandfather Henry about the mouth. A strange, disturbing face. Mary averted her eyes from the portrait and moved towards the door beside which it hung. Her small hand reached out for the latch and jerked it upwards. The door did not budge. It was locked. Oh well. Mary turned away and almost jumped out of her skin as she saw a small, skinny woman peering at her from the angle of the passage. The woman was not of her household and must belong to the castle. She was holding a jug of steaming water. She advanced towards Mary and curtsied clumsily, slopping some of the water on to the floor.

"You be the Princess Mary," she stated confidently.

"Yes."

"You be powerful like your mother, God save her."

"You know my mother?" asked Mary, surprised.

"Aye, and your father too, the blessed Prince Arthur, God assoil him."

Mary's grey eyes opened wide. "Prince Arthur is not my father," she protested. "King Henry is my father."

The woman appeared not to notice the interruption. "Aye, aye," she said, "I mind well when thy father and mother came to Ludlow. New wed they was. Went to bed in that very chamber." The old woman pointed a shaking forefinger at the locked door and cackled with laughter. More water dribbled out of the jug, now supported by only one frail brown hand. "A saucy young rascal 'un was," the woman went on. "In the morning he called for a cup of wine. 'I have been in Spain this night my masters,' he says, 'and 'tis thirsty work'." Here the old woman's mirth got the better of her and placing the jug on the floor she held her sides and rocked with laughter.

Mary began to feel frightened. She did not understand the woman's bawdy talk. The crone came nearer and she shrank back against the cold stone wall of the passage. Old, bloodshot eyes peered avidly at her. "That marriage was consummated right enough, for all the Pope's Bulls saying it weren't," she said. "I was one of them swore she were a virgin, but I was well paid for my pains and I needed the money sore, me man being poorly and not fit for labour."

"What is consummated?" whispered Mary, snatching at the one sinister-sounding word in the old woman's ramblings.

Black, broken teeth grinned at her. "Why, lady, 'tis when a man holds a woman in bed and his private parts swell fit to burst until he . . ." She broke off, mumbling, as a high, female voice shouted at her "Peg! Be off with you now and fill the basins in all the chambers. The princess and her ladies want to cleanse themselves."

Mary, dazed and bewildered, looked with gratitude at the plump figure of Susan Clarencieux, her newest lady-in-waiting, a round-faced rosy girl with curly brown hair. Susan was fifteen and mature beyond her years. She had sized up the situation in an instant and taking the trembling princess in her arms began to comfort her. "Did the silly old crone startle you?" she murmured into the red-gold hair.

"Yes, she startled me," gasped Mary ."Sh . . . she said such strange things."

"Pay them no mind, your grace," advised Susan briskly. "She is half out of her wits like the rest of the old dotards here. She seemed slightly less addle-pated than the other serving-woman so I sent her for the water."

Mary rested her aching head against Susan's well-developed bosom. She was feeling better already. "She said mother's marriage to Prince Arthur had been con . . . er con something. I have forgot the word."

Susan stiffened and the blood drained from her face. She clutched Mary to her but said nothing. She remembered her own mother telling her that the King had only been allowed to marry the Princess Catherine because her marriage to Prince Arthur had not been consummated. If this little tale got about it could cause untold trouble.

Later, after she had seen the princess down the stairs and in the care once more of the other ladies, Susan reported the incident to the Countess of Salisbury. That lady's generous mouth was white-circled with fear as she asked, "Can I trust you to say naught of all this, Susan?"

"On my life," promised Susan stoutly.

The countess believed her and heaved a sigh of relief. "My thanks to you, Susan. Thou'rt a sensible lass."

For the remainder of that day the countess went about her duties with a worried frown creasing her brow. She recalled how distraught Catherine had been at Mary's departure for Ludlow and wondered fearfully if old Peg had spoken the truth when she said that Prince Arthur had consummated his marriage. Catherine, she knew, was quite capable of taking such a secret with her to the grave.

Inevitably, Mary questioned her aunt about the locked chamber. " 'Tis full of old furniture, beds, chests and the like," the countess told her.

"Was it my lady mother's chamber, and did she lay there with my uncle?"

"No, no, methinks she had some other chamber in . . ."

Disconcertingly, for normally her manners were impeccable, the child interrupted her. "What was that word the old woman used? I had it straight and then I forgot. I should like to know what it means. Con . . . something. Constituted? . . . Consecrated?"

" 'Tis naught that need concern you. Now, it is time to take the air."

Mary gave up. She had learned from experience that it was little use trying to cajole grown-ups into telling you something they had decided to keep from you. Resignedly, she went to find her cloak.

The next day the countess took immediate steps to have old Peg pensioned off and dismissed.

3

Dressed in a gown of sombre grey silk, Mary was at her lessons in the castle solar. The gown made her feel dull, as did the old-fashioned gable hood which the countess had made her wear because she said it was the only one that matched the gown. As if it mattered anyway thought Mary irritably. There was no one save dreary old Master Featherstone and her ladies to see her. Involuntarily her right hand sought for the Emperor's emerald ring. It was two years now since the Cardinal had made her send it back to him and still she had not forgotten. Still would her fingers stray in search of that enormous gem which she had loved to caress. Perhaps it would have been better after all if the King had allowed her to go to Spain. Then might the Emperor have hesitated before breaking their betrothal. At eleven Mary had but a dim memory of the frightened child of six who feared to leave her parents.

The hot July sun streamed through the high mullioned windows, illuminating the pages of the book of Latin exercises which the princess had open before her. Master Featherstone, her tutor, hovered over her, a sober, black-gowned figure, stout and solemn-eyed.

" 'Eventide' by Virgil," Mary read tonelessly. *"Nox erat, et placidum carpebant fess soporem. Corpora per terras, silvaeque et saeva quierant . . ."*

"Translate, if you please, your grace," ordered Master Featherstone peremptorily.

Mary sighed and pressed her fingers to her temples. Her head was beginning to ache again and the words swam before her pricking eyes. "It is night . . ." she began.

"Was. Was night," corrected Master Featherstone severely.

"Was night," repeated Mary dutifully, ". . . and round the world . . ."

". . . over the earth." Master Featherstone tut-tutted irritably and fingered the birch switch which lay close to his hand on the table. Mary caught the movement, shivered and looked at the single-handed spring clock fixed to the wall. The hand still had an eighth of an inch to travel before it reached the Roman numeral twelve and she calculated swiftly that it would be at least fifteen minutes before her aunt came to rescue her and take her for her daily walk in the castle grounds. ". . . over the earth," she intoned dully, "weary creatures are enjoying peaceful sleep."

"Were! Were! Were enjoying peaceful sleep!" screamed Master Featherstone and quite forgetting himself he lifted the birch rod high in the air and brought it down with a whistling thwack on Mary's bare hand. He was hot and tired too.

Mary gave a piercing shriek and leapt to her feet. All at once hot Tudor and Spanish blood, running thick in her veins, asserted itself in full measure and she bared her teeth at her tutor. "Varlet!" she insulted him. "How dare you touch my person!"

Instinctively, Master Featherstone recoiled, regarding his

hitherto docile pupil with startled yellow eyes, "Y . . . your lady mother," he stammered. "The . . . the Q . . . Queen said you were to be chastised if you paid no heed to your lessons. She said . . ."

"My lady mother did not mean you to attack me," shouted Mary, "and what of my father? What of the King? Did he say you were to whip me?"

"No . . .er, no, your grace."

"And what if I were tell him that you have dared to lay violent hands upon me? Ho would you like to feel the tormentor's rack stretching your bones and the executioner's axe kissing your fat neck?"

"Your grace!"

Master Featherstone threw up his hands in horror at this unprecedented threat from a child of eleven and the sweat stood out on his temples.

Satisfied that she had gained her point Mary re-seated herself and resumed her translation. ". . . The woods and the wild seas are sunk to rest . . ." she continued.

Master Featherstone did not bother to correct her. His hands were shaking and his mouth was dry. He did not want to lose his place. Three years ago he would have relied on the Queen to defend his every action but of late, if what he heard from court messengers were true, she seemed to be slipping into the background of affairs and it was the King's will which predominated at court. Even the Cardinal was having less to say.

Mary had surprised herself by her own outburst. She had had no intention of frightening poor Master Featherstone. It was just that the rigorous curriculum laid down for her by the Spaniard, Ludovicus Vives, at the request of her mother, had become too much for her, resulting as it did in one headache after another. Today things had seemed more than she could bear and her Tudor temper had got the better of her. Furtively, she glanced up at Master Featherstone and took instant pity on him. He looked so hot in his stuffy black robes and she had been so unkind to him. She redoubled her efforts to translate the exercise correctly and at the end was rewarded by a thin smile from the tutor. Again she looked at the clock. About five minutes. But before she could begin on another exercise, a braying of trumpets from the courtyard announced visitors and pushing aside her books Mary ran to the arrow-slit below the mullioned window, squinting through the narrow, cruciform aperture. "My uncle of

Suffolk," she exclaimed, recognising the heavy, blond-haired figure thirty feet below, "and . . . er, I think 'tis the Earl of Arundel with him."

Master Featherstone was at her side, peering down. "Yes, it must be the Earl of Arundel," he confirmed, "I can see two squires wearing his swallow badge. I wonder what brings them here?"

He was not left long in doubt, for five minutes later the door of the solar flew open and the Countess of Salisbury hurried in, followed by the duke and the earl. Mary ran forward to greet her Uncle Charles, arms outstretched, expecting to be lifted high and heartily bussed. Hurt bewilderment replaced elation when Suffolk arrested her in mid-flight and said quietly, "The King orders your immediate return to London, Mary. Your household here is to be broken up."

Mary's smile wavered. "H . . . how wonderful," she said. "I like it not here anyway and 'tis two years since I saw Mother and Father."

Suffolk and Arundel exchanged glances. Mary felt uneasy. She ran to the countess and buried her head in her aunt's blue brocade gown. Above the child's bowed head the countess looked at Arundel inquiringly. He lifted his eyebrows and shrugged helplessly. He was a very prudent man.

RICHMOND PALACE

June, 1527

I

Mary caught a cold before leaving Ludlow and her aunt insisted that she ride in the leather-curtained litter. "Three weeks in that thing!" moaned Mary. "I shall die of suffocation."

"That you will not," replied the countess firmly, "and you may come out when the rheum leaves you. My jasmine posset should soon take care of it."

Mary sniffed, blew her nose on her kerchief and relapsed into silence. It was fruitless to argue with the countess when she was in one of her mother-hen moods. The litter proved as hot as she had feared and the leather curtains and roof smelt abominably. She endured six days in the close, almost fetid atmosphere, drinking copious draughts of jasmine posset and having to halt the cavalcade for necessary reasons with embarrassing frequency, until the countess pronounced her cold cured and gave orders for her jennet to be saddled.

It was wonderful to be out in the cool, clean air again. Mary's spirits soared. She was going home. Home to the two people whom she loved best. No sense of premonition marred her intense enjoyment of the remainder of that long journey. No disembodied voice whispered in her ear that her safe little world was about to collapse in ruins.

On the twenty-second day after they had left Ludlow Mary spied in the distance the rosy-red bricks of Richmond Palace and so great was her joy at once more beholding that well-known, well-loved place that she bounced up and down in her saddle until the irritated jennet kicked up his back legs in an effort to dislodge the troublesome burden on his back. Mary laughed and clung tightly to the silvery neck. She heeded not her aunt's disapproving glances but spurred forward to ride beside her cousin, Margaret Douglas.

"Almost home, Margaret," she breathed ecstatically.

Margaret's black eyes regarded her cousin with disdain. Such a pother about seeing her parents again. As for her, she'd been only too glad to get away from her mother's sharp tongue and her father's heavy hand which had been wont to rise and fall with monotonous regularity about her ears. But then Mary was still a mere child. No one would think she was eleven. She hadn't even started her moon-times. Margaret, who had experienced two periods felt vastly superior. "You are to be betrothed again," she said abruptly with slight, sarcastic emphasis on the last word.

Mary gasped with surprise. "How can you know that?"

"I heard old Suffolk discussing it with Arundel."

Mary elevated her small, pert nose and said airily, "Oh, I see. You have been listening to idle gossip again, or should I say eavesdropping?"

Margaret reddened at this unpalatable truth and her black eyes snapped angrily. "Just for that I shall not tell you who has been named for you."

"Because you do not know," jeered Mary.

"Oh yes I do. Suffolk said that the King sent Richard Pate as his ambassador to . . ."

"I do not want to know," interposed Mary with dignity and wheeling the jennet rode back to the countess. But she did. She wondered about it for the next half-hour until the gates of the palace appeared through the trees and the trumpets blared on the gatehouse towers.

But she soon forgot her curiosity as she clattered through the gateway into the courtyard and thought that within the space of five minutes she would be clasped in her mother's arms. One of her squires was already holding out his hands to help her dismount and she slid quickly to the ground. Ignoring her aunt's command to, "Wait for me, child!" Mary sped into the palace and hurried towards her mother's apartments. She was stopped on the stairs by Elizabeth Hammond who, after exclaiming at her increased height, told her that her mother was sick of the chicken-pox and could not see her. Such a disappointment after days of joyful anticipation was too much. Mary sat down abruptly on the stairs and dissolved into tears.

Lady Hammond crouched beside her and placed a comforting arm about her shoulders. "The Queen will soon be amended," she promised the girl gently. "Meanwhile she has bid me tell you that she will dictate written messages for you daily until the infection has passed and she can send for you in person."

Mary kneaded her streaming eyes with a grubby fist and smiled up at Lady Hammond. "Have you one for me now?"

Lady Hammond smiled back, nodded and produced from her sleeve a square of parchment. Mary seized it eagerly and began to read—

'Dearest daughter, Welcome home! I am penning this note against your coming to be put into your hands immediately upon your arrival at the palace. As you will have been informed, thy poor old mother is in sad case at the moment but amending swiftly. I would that I could see you, my sweetheart, after all this time, but it would not do for you to catch the pox and spoil that pretty face. Thy father has some happy news for thee. He will tell thee of it anon.

God have thee in His keeping,
Thy loving mother, Catherine R.'

Mary sighed happily as she finished reading her mother's letter. It had cheered her considerably. She guessed, from her conversation with Margaret Douglas, that her father's news would be about her betrothal. Again she wondered who had been named for her and almost wished that her pride had not prevented her from allowing Margaret to finish what she had been going to say to her. "Where is my father?" she asked Lady Hammond.

A faint shadow passed over Lady Hammond's handsome features, but she managed to laugh naturally enough. "Where else but hunting in this fine summer weather?" she answered. "He will be back soon and right glad to see you I doubt not."

Henry was pleased to see his daughter, but she was quick to sense a subtle change in him. He was thinner, less boisterous, a trifle withdrawn. He stood before her in the long gallery, legs arrogantly astride, clad in his favourite hunting green. His gentlemen clustered about him, bright as peacocks. Shrewsbury, Pembroke, Bedford, Exeter and Norfolk eyed the princess curiously.

"You are grown, daughter," said Henry, releasing her from a rather loose embrace.

Mary stepped back slowly, disappointed by the slight coolness of her reception. "Yes, Father."

"You have seen your mother?"

"She would not let me come to her chamber lest I take the chicken-pox."

Henry grunted. "I have an offer for your hand," he said shortly.

"Mother said you had some news for me. She wrote me a . . ."

" 'Tis from Francis, King of the French," Henry blurted impatiently. "A goodly match. How would you like to be Queen of France?"

Mary was dismayed. Not only was Francis at least twenty years older than herself but surely such a match would not please mother. And yet Catherine had used the term 'happy news' in her letter. Mary did not know what to think. Something of her uncertainty must have mirrored itself on her face for Henry said fretfully, "You will like it well enough when the time comes. Francis keeps a brilliant court. Meanwhile, the French ambassadors are here to see you and I have arranged that you shall appear before them in a masque." He frowned, thrusting his chin forward. "You kept up your dancing at Ludlow I trust?"

"Oh yes, Father."

"Mmm, well," said Henry mournfully, as though he doubted the truth of her assertion, "do your best. The Queen's ladies will tell you all about it and rehearse you in your part."

"Yes, Father."

Henry continued to stare at her oddly and Mary had the unhappy feeling that there was a slight hint of distaste in his glance. She stood, unmoving before him, hoping for some expression of warmth. None came. Henry turned away almost rudely and Mary was left standing alone in the long gallery watching a dozen colourful, retreating backs.

2

Next day Mary sought out her mother's ladies to ask them about the masque. She noticed a host of new faces amongst them and wondered where the old familiar ones had gone. Married most like and retired to their husbands' manors to bear a dozen children. The ladies crowded round her, complimenting her on her increased height and blossoming figure, and she basked in the warmth of their praise, feeling better for the first time since her arrival at Richmond. Her mother was still keeping to her chamber but had promised Mary, in a gay little note, that she would be able to see her within two days.

The ladies explained the masque in detail. They were all to be dressed in Icelandic costume and were to emerge from a cave bearing lighted torches. Mary was to be the central figure and was to dance a galliard.

Mary giggled. "Icelandic costume!" she exclaimed. "How is that fashioned?"

Margaret Isley, a tall, thin girl with saucy green eyes, smiled mischievously. "White satin, your grace, lined with green taffety, and the skirt cut in points to expose the legs."

Mary's eyes grew round. "And I am to dance like that? I shall die of shame! The King said that the French ambassadors would be watching."

"And so they will," put in Elizabeth Hammond. "They have got to tell their master what they are buying."

"Lady Hammond!" shrieked Mary. "How can you say such things?" But she could not forbear to laugh and giggle with the rest of the ladies who were chattering excitedly about the great marriage she was to make. All save one. Mistress Anne Boleyn stood apart from the others, fingering the stuff of the rich, gold brocade gown given to her by the King and watching the little scene being played before her with cynical amusement. Her luminous black eyes held a glint of triumph, for today the King had told her that he was of a mind to divorce his wife and marry her, make her Queen of England, and the child of their love should be heir to the throne. Mistress Boleyn wondered how long it would be before Francis decided that the bastard daughter of a King was not good enough for him.

Mary saw the strange, dark lady standing a little apart from the rest. Shy perhaps? She noticed the slight swelling on her neck above the collar of pearls. Poor lady. She would find it hard to get herself a husband.

3

The day of the masque arrived and Mary was in a fever of excitement. She had seen her mother for the first time since her return to Richmond and their reunion had been joyful and slightly emotional. Mary had spent three hours in her mother's chamber telling her all that had passed during her stay at Ludlow. Something, she knew not what, had prevented her from disclosing the details of her encounter with old Peg. Catherine, for her part, had not questioned Mary about the chambers within the castle. She knew, only too well, what they looked like. She had no wish to be reminded.

"Five Welshmen joined my household when I was at Ludlow," Mary informed her mother, "and they all came back with me to Richmond. They came to Ludlow seeking employment. I interviewed each of them personally," she added proudly.

"That was well done, Mary," said Catherine approvingly. "Welsh blood runs in thy father's veins and 'tis fitting that you should be served by Welshmen."

They had gone on to talk of other matters. Mary's studies, the places in Wales she had visited and other, more domestic trifles. Tentatively, Mary mentioned her forthcoming betrothal to the King of France. "You approve the match, Mother?"

A quick frown, gone in an instant, marred Catherine's brow before she smiled brightly and said, "Yes, my daughter, the match pleases me well and 'tis thy father's wish."

Mary looked relieved. Her first depression over the news of her betrothal to Francis had passed. The idea of becoming Queen of France was beginning to appeal to her. "Aunt Mary Tudor was Queen of France," she said dreamily. "She said the court there was wonderful."

Yes, but she was not the sensitive plant you are, my sweetheart, thought Catherine sorrowfully. She did not mind being married to a man three times her age whom she killed with too much loving within eight months of the marriage day, so that she could run off with young Charles Brandon, her first love.

The artful baggage. She'd had it all planned from the first. Had used secret potions most like. Catherine feared for her daughter. Everyone knew that Francis was riddled with the French disease. But she dared not give tongue to her fears. Not now. Mary, like others before her, including Catherine herself, was to be a mere pawn in the hands of politically ambitious kings.

Aloud Catherine said, "It is time to dress for the masque, sweetheart. Get you gone now and come later to bid me good night."

Catherine proffered a cool cheek and Mary kissed her fervently. "How glad I am to see you again, Mother."

"And I you, my daughter. Now hurry, hurry."

When Mary had gone Catherine wiped away a tear and signed to her ladies to bring her black-work embroidery. She wondered uneasily whether the child had sensed anything amiss yet.

4

Mary had ordered Susan Clarencieux to lay out her costume and head-tire in the little chamber adjacent to the great hall at Richmond which was scarcely more than a closet really but which had become known as the 'Princess Mary's chamber' because it was there that she always changed when she was to appear in a masque. It was, by custom, reserved exclusively for her use. She hurried away from her mother's apartments, unaccompanied by any ladies. They were all below, changing for the masque. Palace guards smiled and saluted her as she passed and one, more elderly than the rest, who remembered her as a babe in arms, murmured, " 'Tis grand to see your grace once more!"

Impulsively Mary stopped and took his hand in hers. "And 'tis good to be back, John," she answered.

The sentry's eyes brimmed as he watched the small, grey-gowned figure skipping away down the passage towards the stairs. She had remembered his name! By Jesu, she had remembered! Tudors. Dear God, but they knew how to get to the heart of a man.

Sounds of rustling cloth came from the little chamber and Mary smiled. Dear Susan, she was probably still fussing over her costume without a thought for her own. But when Mary pushed open the door she stopped short, taken aback, for there, almost naked, save for a transparent shift of French lawn, stood the strange lady, her glossy black hair falling to her knees. The lady did not curtsy and Mary felt her cheeks begin to burn. Anger replaced embarrassment and she demanded hotly, "What are you doing here, lady?"

"I might ask the same of you." The smouldering, slightly protuberant eyes, regarded Mary insolently and the thick, winged brows rose inquiringly.

"This is my chamber," declared Mary stoutly. "I always change for masques in here."

"Do you so?"

All at once Mary felt awkward and gauche and just a little afraid. The strange lady was so obviously in command of the situation and it was she who felt like the intruder. She was standing, wondering what to say next, when her father came into the chamber and failing to notice her presence, half-hidden as she was behind the open door, advanced on the lady and buried his gold head in her naked breasts. Over his shoulder Anne Boleyn looked at Mary with sly amusement. The corners of her petulant mouth curved upwards.

Horrified, Mary gazed on the unbelievable, her father making love to a light lady under the same roof that sheltered her mother. Mary knew, of course, that there were certain ladies with whom the King passed the time in his country manors and she knew also that somehow—she was not quite sure of the process involved—young Henry, Duke of Richmond, her half-brother, had been the result of one of these 'friendships', but never, never, had it been known for the King to insult the Queen by conducting an affair at court.

Before Henry could become too amorous Anne drew his attention to the fact that his daughter was present. Startled, he turned and confronted Mary. The ruddy hue of his cheeks deepened and he frowned distractedly. Suddenly he shrugged, and addressing Anne muttered, "She might as well know now as later. Make haste with your dressing and I will speak with her alone."

Smiling, Anne obeyed and withdrew in a swirl of scarlet silk, leaving behind her a heady wave of violet perfume.

When she had gone, shutting the door behind her, Henry's stiff manner relaxed a little and sitting down on a convenient stool he beckoned Mary towards him. She came, a trifle diffidently, still bewildered by the odd little scene she had witnessed. Strong hands pulled her down and then she was sitting on Henry's knee as she had in the old days. There was silence for a moment or two. Henry broke it by saying carefully, "Mary, you love your mother do you not?"

Mary was surprised by this unnecessary question. "Yes, Father, very much."

"Well then, if you love her you will perhaps be able to help her to see what is best for her?"

"What is best for her?" repeated Mary stupidly.

"Yes. You see, sweetheart, I have discovered, to my infinite grief, that God does not look upon my marriage to your mother at all favourably. I read recently in the Book of Leviticus these words"—here Henry fumbled in his sleeve and produced a scrap of parchment which he always carried on his person these days and to which he made frequent reference though he knew its contents by heart. He squinted at his own handwriting, gave a small, prefatory cough and began solemnly, "'And if a man shall take his brother's wife, it is an unclean thing; he hath uncovered his brother's nakedness; they shall be childless'." Three black lines had been scored so deeply under the last four words that they had come through to the other side.

Henry folded the parchment, replaced it in his sleeve and said gravely, "I am firmly convinced, Mary, that this is why we have no son. Now, if God is displeased, there is only one thing I can do to remedy matters. I have therefore applied to Pope Clement that our marriage be annulled in order that I may take someone else to wife and beget a male heir for England."

"The strange lady," murmured Mary involuntarily and with sudden insight.

"Eh? What said you?" Henry's voice was sharp.

"N . . . naught, Father," replied Mary dismally. Her head began to ache and she was so stunned by her father's words that coherent thought was difficult. "Father," she protested weakly, "the Pope gave his blessing for you to marry mother did he not? Aunt Margaret told me that. She said that the marriage vows twixt a man and a woman are absolutely binding . . ." Mary burst into tears. "Oh Jesu, Father, you can't mean what you say. Why did you let all these years pass before . . . ?" She choked on her sobs and coughed miserably.

Henry realised for the first time that his daughter was no longer a child. She had seized on the one salient fact which would always be held against him. Patting her back clumsily he began to plead with her. She must see that he needed a son. He loved her dearly, of course, but the English would never take kindly to a woman ruler. He must have a son. And her mother would not suffer. She was not in the best of health anyway and the peace of a convent . . . Henry broke off as Mary's sobs increased in intensity and she gasped between gulps, "No, no, Father, not a convent . . . Wh . . . what about my brother Henry? C . . . Could you not make him your heir?"

"He is a bastard," said Henry flatly. He was becoming impatient with her.

Mary dabbed at her red eyes and made one last effort. "Aunt Margaret says that mother and Prince Arthur were only children when they were wed and that such a marriage does not count. That old woman at Ludlow was wrong when she said they shared the same chamber and . . ." Mary jumped with fright as Henry bellowed at her, "And what? And what? What old woman? What did she tell you?"

Unceremoniously he set Mary on her feet, rose, placed both hands on her shoulders and shook her slightly. "Now, Mary, what did the woman say? What? What?" The shaking increased and Mary's teeth chattered in her head. She was confused. "I . . . I don't remember exactly. Aunt Margaret said she was half out of her wits. I . . ."

"Try! Try to remember," urged Henry and his grey eyes, reduced to mere slits, probed her now terrified face.

With sudden intuition Mary realised that Henry was trying to force out of her knowledge which would damage her mother. She would give her life rather than that this should happen. "I cannot remember, Father," she said stubbornly. "The old woman frightened me and I knew not what she said."

He did not know whether to believe her or not, but the determined thrust of her chin and the hard line of her mouth told him he would get nothing further from her at the moment. With an exclamation of disgust he turned away, pushing her from him, and strode from the chamber. Mary looked down at her crumpled white satin dress. Henry had been sitting on it.

5

The masque was a dismal failure. The torches went out, the cave collapsed, the greyhounds urinated on the artificial trees and the French ambassadors were unimpressed and commented too loudly that Mary was scrawny and not yet ready for marriage. The ambassadors had received sealed instructions from their master, Francis I, not to conclude the marriage negotiations, for a certain secret matter appertaining to the King of England was being bruited abroad.

Mary did not care that the betrothal came to naught. Her thoughts now were all for her mother. She wandered about the court, a small, disconsolate figure, ignored by her father and worried over by her mother. She went to Mass often, turning to the one Being from whom she could derive solace, and it was during this early period of her unhappiness that her deep religious sense developed and grew so that in the end she lost the ability to compromise with human frailty.

Catherine never mentioned the word divorce to Mary and wisely Mary refrained from broaching the subject herself.

For Catherine divorce did not exist. Henry was bewitched and she must wait patiently until the spell was broken.

The King questioned every member of Mary's household, including the countess, about the woman who had frightened her. None save the countess and Susan Clarencieux knew anything of such a woman and these two remained grimly and loyally silent. Both realised that the secret was even more dangerous now that the King's mind was turning towards divorce. His 'secret matter' was being openly discussed about the court. The word 'divorce' hung on the air like a threatening plague miasma. But a divorce was not an easy thing to come by, even for a King as mighty as Henry. It necessitated more than the publication of Papal Bulls and the comfortable disposal of an unwanted wife in a convent. If the wife was in no mind to be banished and the Pope, very much under the thumb of Catherine's nephew the Emperor Charles, in no mind to banish her, there was little the King could do.

The weary months dragged by. Wolsey laboured long and hard on his master's behalf, was disgraced and died in the attempt, having achieved less than nothing. Henry continued to plague Mary to tell him of the incident at Ludlow. She remained obdurate and so, soon after the Cardinal's bones had been laid to rest at Leicester Abbey the King, his patience exhausted, did the thing he knew would hurt Mary most. He separated her from her mother. Mary was sent to his manor in Newhall in Essex and Catherine to Ampthill, near Woburn, a damp, desolate place with its broken park pales and weed-infested gardens.

Mary was never to see her mother again.

PART TWO

"When in disgrace with fortune and men's eyes,
I all alone beweep my outcast state,
And trouble deaf heaven with my bootless cries,
And look upon myself and curse my fate . . ."

Shakespeare's *Sonnets.*

NEWHALL AND GREENWICH

September, 1533

I

Mary spent three long, miserable years at Newhall Manor, during which time she turned from a child into a woman. She was seventeen and a half now, and although she had grown several inches since her return from Ludlow, she was possessed of the same thin child's face with its serious grey eyes under finely arched brows, its small retroussé nose and firm, delicate mouth with the tucked-in corners. At a time when, as the daughter of a powerful King, she should have been looking forward to a brilliant marriage, she sat about the dreary manor, still pursuing her interminable studies and practising on her lute, a shabby little figure in a brown fustian gown, for now she had no money with which to buy the velvets and silks she loved so much.

At first her father had allowed her to write to her mother, still lodged at Ampthill, but later, when he found he could not bully her into telling him about the affair at Ludlow he forbade all intercourse between them and their letters ceased. Mary was left in dismal ignorance of the state of her mother's health which she feared to be poorly. In the early days too Henry came often to Newhall and always would he interrogate her, making her stand before him for as much as an hour at a time while he fixed her with that baleful grey stare she had come to dread so much and bombarded her with a veritable cannonade of questions. Close behind the King would stand Thomas Cromwell, the solid black lump of a man who had taken Wolsey's place in Henry's counsels. A clever, scheming, ambitious man was Thomas Cromwell, as devoted to the King's interests as ever his master and mentor Wolsey had been.

To her surprise Mary sensed in him a certain sympathy for her plight, but she knew that that same sympathy would never prompt him to come out openly on her side. After one of these fruitless interviews Henry would go away, his brow dark with displeasure, and it might be another month or even three before she saw him again. It had become a point of pride with Mary never to disclose what she had learned at Ludlow, for at seventeen she realised the implications of what old Peg had told her. Sometimes when she lay, sleepless and brooding, in the small hours, Mary would fancy that she could hear the cracked old voice—"that marriage was consummated right enough, for all the Pope's Bulls saying it weren't"—and now she remembered the word she had found so elusive at Ludlow. It was on everybody's tongue. She was still not quite sure what it meant. She knew only that if a marriage had been consummated it was absolutely indissoluble. It was the one bright spot in Mary's life that she had it in her power to protect her mother. Henry would never understand that his continual pestering of his daughter had the sole result of hardening her determined resolve to withstand his bullying at all costs.

The King obtained his divorce, helped by a brilliant little mouse of a cleric called Thomas Cranmer, whose suggestion that the universities of Europe be consulted on the question of the King's divorce put him high in the royal favour and resulted finally in the breach with Rome. At Cranmer's prompting Henry declared himself Supreme Head of the Church in England, thus severing the last restricting tie which bound him to his unwanted wife. Early in 1533 he married Anne Boleyn, newly created Marchioness of Pembroke, kinswoman to the great Howard family, having first, very wisely, made her pregnant. It would never have done, after his six-year fight for freedom, if he had married a barren woman. That would have been irony indeed. In 1533, old Archbishop Warham having died the previous year, Thomas Cranmer was made Archbishop of Canterbury and obligingly pronounced Henry's marriage to Queen Catherine invalid. In May of the same year Henry's new Queen was crowned at Westminster wearing Catherine's jewels.

At Newhall Mary heard the news with horror. A tight knot of fear gripped her belly. The breach with Rome made her feel very vulnerable. If her father could achieve thus much to gain his ends, of what further deeds would he be capable? Her fear would have turned to terror had she been able to foresee just what Henry would do in the coming months to uphold his actions.

Late in August Mary received a summons to come to Greenwich for the new Queen's lying-in. She was still heiress-presumptive to the throne and it was therefore her duty to be present at the birth of a possible male heir. The Countess of Salisbury, the only one of her ladies who had been allowed to remain with her when she left court three years before, was to go with her, together with the usual complement of lower household servants.

Mary brooded over the summons and discussed it with the countess. "I am half-inclined not to go," she declared with a pathetic assumption of defiance. "The lady Anne is sure to give me the sharp end of her tongue." Mary would have cut out her own tongue rather than dignify Anne Boleyn with the title of Queen.

The countess, still the same vigorous old lady of yore, replied swiftly, "You must go, child. There will be trouble else." She rose from her stool by the window, allowing the altar cloth she was embroidering to drop from her lap to the floor, and came to where Mary was standing by the felt-draped table idly leafing through a book of Greek verse. She placed a comforting, skinny arm about the girl's narrow shoulders and gave her a little squeeze. " 'Twill not be so bad," she assured her. "You will only have to be present in the chamber at the moment of birth to verify the sex of the child and then you may be gone. All will be over quickly and judging from my own experience in such matters the lady will be in no case to twit you."

Mary forgot her own troubles for the moment in sudden sympathy for her aunt. "I sometimes forget that you have children of your own, aunt," she said. "You never see them, shut up as you are here with me, and now that Reginald is gone abroad you must miss him sorely."

Henry had been anxious to have Reginald Pole, now in Holy orders, on his side over the divorce question, and had tried to bribe him with the offer of the archbishopric of York, vacant since Wolsey's death, but in a stormy interview with the King, Pole had been so outspoken in Catherine's favour that Henry had struck him. The quarrel was patched up and Henry had later given Pole permission to go abroad to Avignon.

In response to Mary's remark the countess gave a little sigh but said, with her usual practical common sense, "Reginald is safer at Avignon. I am glad that he is not at court. He is too forthright. I warrant his tongue would have landed him in the Tower ere now."

Mary could find no reply to this doleful truth. She found her place in the Greek verse and was just about to seat herself at the table to read when a page knocked and entered.

He bowed to both ladies and addressing Mary said breathlessly, "The Spanish ambassador, Messire Chapuys, is below, your grace and wishes to have speech with you."

Mary and the countess exchanged puzzled glances and Mary said at once, "Send Messire Chapuys up, Stephen." She barely had time to sit down, adjust her hood and smooth her gown before the small, black-haired figure of a young Savoyard appeared in the doorway bowing low. His soft, alert brown eyes sought Mary's and he advanced towards her with a sort of bouncing gait characteristic of him. Eustace Chapuys, a young man of twenty-three, was new in the service of the Emperor Charles and took his duties very seriously. A volatile, intelligent youth, he had been chosen by Charles for this important post because of his uncanny ability for obtaining information without disclosing in return anything of importance concerning his master. With the situation in England as it was at present Charles needed someone like this, for there were many secrets to be learned at the court. Chapuys' single fault was that he tended to become over-excited, sensing danger and conspiracy in every look and glance which passed between Henry and his ministers. Time and experience taught him to control this tendency.

Mary, though at a loss to know why he had come, was glad to see him and rose from her stool to give him greeting. She liked Chapuys who treated her with the utmost respect as befitted her high rank, and yet conversed in a warm, friendly manner so that she felt at ease in his presence. "What brings you here, Messire?" she asked, smiling at him. She thought of her mother and her lips trembled. "N . . . not the Queen I trust? I know she is in poor health and . . ."

"No, no, your grace," Chapuys hastened to reassure her. Somewhat belatedly he straightened his creased doublet and smoothed his hair. He had been hurrying, having ridden all the way from Greenwich in four hours. "I came because I heard of the summons which your grace has received to attend the birth of the lady Anne's child"—Chapuys was someone else who never referred to Anne as Queen—"and to give you warning that you should take your own taster to court."

The countess, who had resumed her stitching, looked up sharply.

"M . . . My taster?" queried Mary puzzledly.

"Yes, your grace, so that you may be assured that what

you eat has not been . . . er, tampered with," Chapuys finished delicately.

Mary's expression was blank. "Poisoned, you mean, Messire?"

"Yes."

"But who would wish to do such a dreadful thing to me. I mean I do not understand . . . I . . ." Mary faltered, biting her lip to keep it from trembling.

Chapuys shrugged bony, eloquent shoulders and fiddled with the bunch of aglets which decorated his black velvet doublet. He decided that he could not dissemble on so vital a matter. "The King, your grace," he said quietly.

"My father?" Mary's voice rose a whole octave before she threw back her head and rocked with slightly hysterical laughter.

Chapuys regarded her gravely and all at once Mary stopped laughing. Her eyes searched his sombre face. "You . . . you cannot mean it, Messire," she stammered. "Why, the idea is monstrous absurd . . . is it not?" Her heart began to beat faster and the strength seemed to drain from her legs. She put out a hand and gripped the edge of the table. She had the peculiar and frightening sensation that she was standing outside herself watching the enactment of a strange little scene which bore no relation to the Princess Mary of England. Without apparent volition her mind went back to the last occasion when her father had visited her to ply her with his nagging questions. He had been badly out of humour and before he had left her he had thrown one last, sinister remark over his shoulder at her which, at the time, Mary had put down to his bad temper. "Take care you do not try me too far, my girl. There is a limit, even to my patience. Others before me have known how to deal with plaguey brats." Others before him? Had he meant . . .? Oh, Blessed Virgin, no! He could not have meant his great-uncle, King Richard the Third, who had had his own nephews murdered in the Tower? These and other dark, disturbing thoughts raced through Mary's mind as she continued to regard Chapuys' serious young face with its over-long nose. She noticed inconsequentially the hair-sprouting wart which clung to the side of his mouth like a witch's mark.

Seeing her consternation Chapuys went on hastily, "Of course, your grace, the King may merely try to marry you off to some low fellow to be rid of you. That is something else you must avoid at all costs."

Mary sat down abruptly in her chair, put her head in her hands and murmured absently, "Go you below, Messire, and refresh yourself. I will order my Steward to wait on you in the hall. What you have said has greatly disturbed me. I must have time to think." But when he had gone Mary rose again and with brimming eyes moved blindly towards the countess who crushed her head protectively to her breast.

2

Mary made the journey to Greenwich in apprehensive mood, exchanging hardly a word with the countess on the way. A fine September drizzle soaked her through to the skin, but she would not seek the shelter of her litter. Only the cool air could cleanse away her festering thoughts. The small, bedraggled cavalcade reached Greenwich at four in the afternoon, their longing to change into dry clothes making them cover the last mile in fifteen minutes. About the palace, which was crowded to capacity, there was an air of lively expectancy. All the great nobles and their ladies, as well as quite a few country knights with their wives, as many as could be accommodated, had flocked to Greenwich to be present at the birth. To Mary had been allotted a small chamber, not more than eight feet square, on the second floor of the palace. The countess was obviously expected to share the chamber with her, for two truckle beds, topped by dirty, straw-filled mattresses, had been carelessly erected and shoved together against the wall. There was no sign of any bed coverings.

In a towering rage the countess descended to the lower regions to find the Steward. She protested strongly to him about the inadequacy of the accommodation and furnishings which were. she said, entirely unbefitting the Princess Mary's high station. The Steward's reply to her angry outburst was like a douche of icy water in her face. "The chamber has been selected for the accommodation of the Lady Mary, the King's bastard daughter, by the Queen's grace."

White-lipped the countess demanded, "Where is the King? I would have speech with him."

"At Richmond, Madam," replied the Steward calmly.

"His grace has taken a small party of his gentlemen on a hunting expedition. He will not return until after the birth has taken place."

The countess felt the blood drain from her face. "Th . . . the King is at Richmond?" she repeated faintly. If this were so it looked very much as if Chapuys' fears for Mary's safety were well founded. It would be typical of Henry to arrange that some accident befall the child and to make sure that he was nowhere near enough to become involved in it. The countess had never had any great fondness for Henry. She suspected that the brash, swaggering exterior masked a hidden streak of cowardice in the royal make-up. Silently she called herself to task. She must not allow her dislike of Henry to influence her judgement. Chapuys was an imaginative young man. Henry would never poison his own daughter. Then why, she asked herself, did you advise the child to heed Chapuys' warning and bring her taster to Greenwich? Oh, Jesu, what a broil. Distractedly, the countess dismissed the Steward and returned to her charge.

When Mary and her aunt descended to the hall for the evening meal most of the company was already assembled. Many high-ranking nobles with their ladies were seated about the board, faces Mary knew so well. Norfolk was there with his duchess, Elizabeth Stafford. Elizabeth Tilney, now the dowager-duchess, had been forbidden the court because of her tactless comments on the King's divorce. Arundel was beside Norfolk with his countess. Then came Exeter, Northampton, Hastings, Suffolk and Henry, Duke of Richmond, her half-brother. Mary saw that they were all still dressed in purple mourning for her Aunt Mary Tudor who had died in July of congestion of the lung. As she entered the hall not a single figure rose to curtsy to her and hot tears sprang to her eyes. There was an embarrassed greeting here and there and Exeter was man enough to defy the prevailing wind by calling loudly, "Welcome, little Mary. I vow thou'rt grown beyond recognition." Mary smiled weakly at him and sought for her place. The Steward bustled forward and conducted her to a place far down the central board so that she found herself surrounded by unfamiliar knights from the shires. The countess was about to follow her when the Steward halted her progress and pointed to a vacant place beside the Countess of Arundel. It was the biggest insult Mary had yet been made to suffer. The countess shrugged off the Steward's prompting arm and went to sit beside Mary, shoving savagely at the buxom wife of a Norfolk knight. The lady moved her ample bottom along the bench with remarkable celerity. The Countess of Salisbury was a very great lady, a royal Plantagenet no less. She would have food for gossip for the rest of her days. Lesser folk at the other boards along the sides of the hall watched the scene with interest, glad that they had no part in the troubled affairs of the great.

Mary's taster was in place behind her chair and the covered dishes were being brought into the hall, when there was a fresh commotion at the door, a braying of trumpets and to everyone's shocked amazement the Queen, heavy with child, entered. It was unprecedented for the Queen to appear in public when she was so near her time, but Anne was a commoner and made her own rules. Walking with extreme care, she took her place on the raised dais, hitherto empty, it being reserved solely for the King and Queen and whoever was in attendance for the day. Anne was accompanied by the Marchionesses of Exeter and Northampton, Madge Shelton, her cousin, Lady Shelton, her aunt, Viscountess Rochford, the wife of her brother, George Boleyn and three other ladies, one a pale, blue-eyed blonde called Jane Seymour who had served Queen Catherine. Jane had wanted to leave court when Catherine was sent away, but she had two very ambitious brothers who were determined that she should serve the new Queen. The King not being present, no gentlemen took their places on the dais.

Everyone rose and bowed to the Queen and the meal began. The talk in the hall increased in volume until it was necessary to shout at one's nearest neighbour to be heard. As the first dish was served and Mary's platter filled by a servant, her taster leaned forward, and selecting a portion of fish, speared it on the end of a silver dagger. A shrill voice, rising well above the babble in the hall, effectively silenced the noisy company. "What fear you, lady?" called Anne. "That you will be poisoned?" The question was followed by a peal of derisive laughter.

Mary gazed dumbly in the Queen's direction. At seventeen her sight had deteriorated considerably through long hours at her books and all she could see of Anne was a blur of blue silk and the gleam of rubies set in a gold head-tire. "Why should anyone want to poison you?" queried the insistent voice. "A bastard is scarce important enough to be disposed of. What say you, Richmond?" The young Duke of

Richmond giggled feebly and plunged his nose in his wine goblet to cover his embarrassment.

Not a hand moved in the silent hall. Chicken legs, arrested half-way to mouths by the unexpected interruption, hung poised in the air like so many question marks, mouths drooped slackly open. Anne's taunting manner gave way to vicious anger. "The meal has already been assayed," she snapped. "Dismiss that fellow on the instant!"

Mary felt the comforting pressure of her aunt's hand on her arm. She turned to look at the countess who nodded imperceptibly and with a feeble wave of her hand Mary sent the taster away. Cheeks burning, eyes fixed miserably on her platter, she commenced to eat her fish. But Anne had not yet finished with her. Had not yet humiliated her enough, this troublesome brat whose lineaments and bearing irritatingly proclaimed her Tudor and royal through and through. "Since you are so chary of eating your food, lady," she called stridently, "perhaps you will not mind attending me. Lady Willoughby, who usually holds my napkin for me, is sick of a fever. You may take her place."

Gasps of incredulity, quickly suppressed, rippled round the board. It was unthinkable that a princess of the blood royal should be made to hold the napkin into which the Queen was wont to spit particles of food which she rejected. The lady who performed this rather unpleasant office was generally well-born but she would not rank as high as a princess, a duchess or even a countess. Mary hesitated, uncertain what to do and even her aunt seemed at a loss. She sensed curiosity, hostility and sympathy in varying degrees all about her. Her eye was caught by that of Thomas Cromwell, seated higher up the board. He nodded briefly at her. The nod was accompanied by a slight shrug of the shoulders as if to say, "You must accept the inevitable. You have no choice." Inwardly, Mary reproached Chapuys for making her look such a fool with his over-exaggerated fears of poison. She wished that he was present that she might give him a tongue-lashing and relieve her feelings after this nightmare was over, but he had gone to the King at Richmond.

In the end, native common sense came to Mary's aid. She was vastly outnumbered. This was not the time for a demonstration of defiance. The fight would be continued later. Slowly she rose from the bench and walked with deliberately measured tread to the foot of the dais. She dropped the

Queen too low a curtsy, an imitation of the mock obeisance people accorded the Lord of Misrule at the Christmas festivities. Only the countess, who knew her so well, sensed the implied insult. Mary mounted the two velvet-draped steps and went to stand beside the Queen. Catherine Tilney, one of Anne's Howard relations, silently handed her a large white napkin. Mary shook it to release it from its folds and draping it over her hands held it before her.

"Hold it nearer, girl," commanded Anne sharply. "I may want to spit at any moment. This cursed fish is full of bones."

The meal proceeded. The silence in the hall was broken by a subdued murmur of talk which quickly rose to a rumbling roar as everyone resumed interrupted conversations. Course after course was eaten, gallons of wine were poured down dry throats, the minstrels in the gallery played the latest airs and Mary, the small brown figure standing still as a statue beside the glittering Queen, was temporarily forgotten. She stood there for an hour, suffering sly, unfriendly glances from Anne's ladies who were mostly related to the new Queen, and owed their places to her astonishing rise to favour.

At last Anne turned towards her, black eyes gleaming maliciously, mouth bulging. Mary's stomach heaved as she braced herself to receive the contents of the royal mouth. Though used to the eating habits of the court she had never approved of the way food was arbitrarily discharged into napkins. It seemed to her a disgusting habit. She had often asked her mother why the King did not put a stop to it.

Anne's head was hovering over the napkin. Suddenly she swallowed hard, clutched her stomach and pitched forward over the table. All her ladies save one ran to her assistance, brushing Mary aside. Mary felt a hand on her arm. She turned to find Jane Seymour at her elbow. "Serve her right," Jane whispered into Mary's ear. "Her time has come. Be of good cheer, your grace. I doubt not but in time all will amend itself." Then she was gone and fussing about the Queen with the other ladies. Mary felt slightly heartened. She looked down at the body of the hall. She was able to discern a number of upturned faces nodding and smiling at her. Not a few present had been disgusted by Anne's treatment of her. It was good to know that she had some friends.

3

Mary sat in the Queen's ante-chamber fiddling with her rosary. She had been there for over twenty hours. The small chamber was packed with ladies. No one said much to her, some being afraid to speak with her, others too busy to bother. The moans from the bedchamber were increasing in intensity and Mary's lip curled disdainfully. What could one expect from a commoner? She'd wager her own dear mother had not opened her lips the whole time she was in labour, save perhaps to ask for a cup of water.

Mary glanced at the elaborate cruciform clock reposing on the close cupboard, with its figure of Christ on the Cross painted in bright enamels below the round dial. Almost half after three o'clock. She wondered how much longer she would have to wait. She wanted only to be gone from Greenwich, the scene of her bitter humiliation, back to the comparative peace of Newhall.

Another five minutes went by and then the door of the bedchamber flew open and the midwife signalled frantically to the ladies that the birth was imminent and that they must come in at once to witness it. And for Jesu's sweet sake to send for the Lord Chancellor.

In the confused scramble that followed Mary was pushed and shoved to the back of the crowd until a calm, clear voice halted the mad rush by saying firmly, "Precedence for the Princess Mary! Precedence!" It was Jane Seymour, and her voice carrying a certain degree of authority, the sea of coloured velvets, brocades and silks parted and Mary was allowed to pass through into the birth chamber first. Thomas Lord Audley, Lord Chancellor, who had been waiting in the closet beyond the ante-chamber, was close on her heels and they were both in time to see the midwife parting mother and child.

Anne Boleyn lay back exhausted. "Is it a boy?" she asked weakly. "Mistress Wickford, is it a boy?" The midwife looked down at the squirming female child in her hands and was silent. Anne's pale, sweat-bedewed eyelids snapped open. The midwife's silence spoke louder than words. "Oh, Jesu, not after all that!" she moaned. "The King will be displeased . . ."

Despite her hatred for the woman, Mary's warm heart stirred with pity as she gazed on the white face resting on the satin pillows, surrounded by the tangled mass of black hair. Her pity was quickly dispelled as the Queen's dark gaze found her face and she rasped, "Make your obeisance to the Princess of Wales, lady!"

Mary stepped back as though she had been slapped and turning, ran from the bedchamber. In her headlong flight she bumped into a small, pale man in clerical robes who put out his hands to steady her. "Thanks, my lord," she gasped and pushed by him. It was some time later before she realised that she had proffered thanks to Thomas Cranmer, the man who had declared her mother's marriage to her father invalid and thus made of her a bastard.

HATFIELD AND ELTHAM

June, 1535–May, 1536

I

Madge Shelton caught Mary a stinging blow across her right ear as she knelt before the small *prie-dieu* in her bed-chamber communing with the Blessed Virgin. As Mary pitched sideways her rosary became entangled in the silver pomander ball at her girdle, the string snapped and the carved ivory beads scattered like peppercorns all over the floor. Trembling with shock, Mary struggled to her feet and faced her tormentor. She put up a cautious hand to feel her ear and it came away speckled with blood, for Madge's finger-rings had bitten into the lobe.

Madge's flat, bony face expressed irritation and her hard blue eyes held no pity for the thin, nervous girl standing before her, whose hands made a continual 'washing' movement below the level of her waist. She stabbed with a thick fore-finger at several strands of tow-coloured hair which had escaped from under her hood as she said sharply, "I thought I bid you change the Princess Elizabeth's gown after Mass? You are here to serve her you know, not just to stand gawping while others do all the work, or wearing out your knees at your everlasting prayers while I and my mother run round and round like spit dogs."

Mary's grey eyes pleaded for understanding. "I . . . I was going to dress the princess Mistress Shelton," she whispered, "but Lady Bryan had not finished washing her and she said I . . ."

"Well, she must have finished by now," said Madge rudely, " 'tis a full hour since Mass and what else you can find to pray about when you've already spent two hours in the chapel I cannot imagine."

"I find comfort in prayer," replied Mary, a small note of defiance creeping into her voice.

"Hah!" snorted Madge contemptuously, "comfort is it? You'll find small comfort, lady, unless you do as you are told and right quickly. Go you now and attend the princess's grace," then, as Mary hesitated, "God's love, girl, get you gone. How many more times have I got to tell you?" Madge looked as though she might be going to raise her hand to strike her another blow and Mary took several steps backwards before saying timidly, "Did you say the gold brocade gown, Mistress Shelton?"

"Yes, yes," answered Madge impatiently, "the gold brocade with the green satin undergown and her red velvet shoes. The princess must look her best to see her father."

Mary's pale face lost its last vestige of colour and her eyes looked enormous. Black smudges bruised the skin below her eyes. "F . . . father is coming here? T . . . today?"

Madge smiled cruelly. "That surprised your ladyship, did it not?"

Mary tried to control the stammer which had become habitual with her of late. "No one told me."

Madge shrugged. "Why should they? The King and Queen are coming to see their daughter, the Princess Elizabeth. It is a purely private visit and does not concern you, my lady. You will keep to your chamber while they are here."

Mary's voice cracked with disappointment. "My father will doubtless wish to see me," she protested pathetically. "He is sure to ask for me. I shall put on my best gown, too." Mary's best gown was a patched and sweat-stained relic, nearly twenty years out of date, which had once belonged to her Aunt Margaret, now married for the third time, to Henry Stewart, Lord Methven. That lady, hearing of her niece's plight, had grudgingly sent it to her from Scotland.

"The King's grace will not see you," persisted Madge harshly. "You should know that well enough. You are a foolish chit. You have only to append your signature to the Oath of Succession and your father will welcome you back to court with loving arms."

"Never!" Mary drew herself up to her full height of five feet one and a half inches and regarded Madge Shelton coldly. This woman might beat and bully her into cowering submission over small domestic matters, but when it came to something like the oath Mary would have died rather than put her name to such an infamous document.

Madge Shelton's blue eyes fell first before the granite gaze of an angry Tudor. She shrugged unconcernedly. " 'Tis your bed you've made. You must lie on it," she said matter-of-factly. Her voice assumed its old bullying manner. "Now get you to the princess. I'll not tell you again."

Silently Mary brushed by her and went to her sister's apartments, her mind in a whirl. Father was coming here today and she was not to be allowed to see him. Dear Jesu, if only she could. If only she could explain to him how she felt. He would understand then. She knew he would. Mary sought for her kerchief in the sleeve of her grey gown and wiped her eyes. She told herself sternly that she must try to hold back the tears which sprang too readily to her eyes. She was for ever weeping these days. Indeed there was very little to laugh about. All the same, she must try to remember that she was a Tudor princess, however badly she was treated.

Mary had been brought to Hatfield Manor in Hertfordshire soon after the birth of the baby princess who had been named after her grandmother, Elizabeth of York. Mary was to serve her half-sister as lady-in-waiting. For almost a year now she had endured nothing but taunts and insults from Lady Shelton, the Queen's aunt, her daughter Madge and the Lady Alice Clere, another of Anne Boleyn's aunts. She was not allowed to go out, either walking or riding, and if she gave offence in any way, however trivial, they would forbid her to go to Mass. The Queen had ordered Madge Shelton to, "give the Lady Mary a box over the ears now and then for the wretched bastard she is," and Madge had not hesitated to do so. Indeed Mary wished that Madge would sometimes strike other parts of her body, but she had taken the Queen's words so literally to heart that Mary was beginning to experience a sort of hollow, ringing sound in both ears which caused her acute distress.

The only friend Mary had in the household was Margaret, Lady Bryan, the Princess Elizabeth's nurse, who had been nurse to Mary herself in happier days. Lady Bryan tried to show her sympathy for Mary in many small ways, by bringing her possets when her head ached and slipping tempting morsels of food up to her bedchamber when she thought herself unobserved. But she had to be careful. She dared not show too much affection for the girl she had nursed through babyhood. When Mary had come to Hatfield all her ladies had been dismissed, including the Countess of Salisbury, who now lived in enforced retirement at her manor of Wimborne in Dorset, contemplating her beehives and her herb garden it is true, but hardly with peace in her heart.

In January, 1534 Mary had been officially bastardised by

Act of Parliament and excluded from the succession which was to devolve on the children of Anne Boleyn. Every member of Parliament was made to swear an oath to observe the conditions of the Act—the Oath of Succession. Brave Bishop Fisher of Rochester and the scholarly Thomas More had both refused to swear and were now lodged in the Tower awaiting trial for high treason. Henry had sent his commissioners to Hatfield with orders to obtain Mary's signature to the oath. She had, of course, refused to sign their papers, and her father's displeasure had been conveyed to her in a letter from Thomas Cromwell. "Thy father, the King's grace, intends to deprive you of the felicity of seeing his person until you be more humble and submissive to his wishes . . ."

Mary sighed as she traversed the passage leading to the nursery. If only she could speak with her father and explain to him why she could not sign the oath. Could not bring herself to admit that her mother's marriage to him was no marriage at all. In the old days, when she was a child, Henry would often take her on his knee to tell her a romantic tale. Always would he emphasise the virtue of loyalty. Loyalty, above all else, was the supreme virtue of the knights of old he would say. Surely he had not forgotten, would see that she must remain true to Catherine? Mary suffered a quick pang of misery as she thought of her mother, immured now in Kimbolton Castle in Huntingdonshire and going in daily fear of being poisoned according to Chapuys.

She entered the nursery to find the baby princess playing happily on the floor with Lady Bryan's work-box. Lady Bryan herself sat placidly stitching a smock by the open window, the day being mild and fair. She greeted Mary kindly, indicating with her needle the tiny gold brocade gown which she had laid out across a stool. She could have dressed the princess herself but knew she would only get Mary into further trouble if she forestalled her in her duties. Mary bent down to tickle Elizabeth under the chin, noting the child's pale skin and sprouting red hair. Henry's grey eyes regarded her curiously and the little plump hands went out to her. She is so like father, thought Mary sadly. She was just about to pick up the child when the chamber door burst open and Madge Shelton bustled in, followed by Lady Shelton, thin as a twig and yellow as an autumn leaf. Both women screamed at Mary in unison, "The King and his party are coming! Get you to your chamber, girl!"

So absorbed had Mary been with the baby that her usually quick ear had missed the dull sound of approaching hoof-beats. She could hear them now though, quite distinctly, and her heart gave a little flutter. Madge was pinching her arm and urging her towards the door. "The dress," protested Mary, desperately playing for time. "The princess is s . . . st . . . still wearing . . ."

"No time for you to do that," piped up Lady Shelton. "Lady Bryan can do it."

So Mary was hustled, willy-nilly, out of the nursery and back to her own bedchamber. Her heart sank as she heard the oak bar being slammed into place outside the door. She ran to the casement which overlooked the courtyard, but the window bay jutted out so far that when the party clip-clopped under the wooden portcullis she was unable to see more than a few feathered velvet bonnets which quickly disappeared through the arched gateway into the inner courtyard. Wearily she removed her unadorned hood of stiffened grey fustian and flung it into the corner of the bedchamber. Then she slumped face downwards on the bed. A sharp piece of straw from the mattress poked through the covering and pricked her shoulder and she started to cry weakly. She had not been in the best of health since she came to Hatfield, being plagued by constant toothache and headaches and tears came easily to her. Sometimes, when she walked in the long gallery, she would feel a curious sort of faintness, accompanied by an overwhelming, irrational fear. Then would her knees buckle and her heart start to thump and she would be glad to seek the shelter of a window seat until the spasm had passed. Life was miserable indeed.

The sound of the bar being removed, followed by a soft knock on the door brought Mary swiftly up to a sitting position and her heart gave a tremendous leap of joy. Father had sent for her! But when she flew to the door and flung it wide her face fell, for there stood Thomas Cromwell, Master of the Rolls. Father would have sent one of his squires to summon her. Cromwell was probably only going to pester her about the oath again. He did, urging her to submission in the gentle, hypnotic voice which was so persuasive.

"I cannot sign the oath, Master Cromwell," said Mary drearily, when the soft voice finished speaking. "You know I cannot."

"You do not want to see your father again then? Return

to the court and take your rightful place amongst the Queen's ladies?" Cromwell's small brown eyes were mildly inquiring.

"Not under those terms," declared Mary stoutly. "And were I to come to court I should expect precedence over my father's mistress, the Lady Anne Boleyn. My rightful place as you call it, Master Cromwell, is as the King's eldest daughter and heiress-presumptive to the throne, not his bastard."

Cromwell did not bother to comment on this spirited outburst. There was really nothing he could say to convince this stubborn girl that she no longer held the high place that had once been hers. "It makes no difference to the King whether you sign or not," he pointed out carefully. "The thing is done by Act of Parliament. You hurt only yourself by refusing to submit. Were you to do so you could have all the fine clothes and jewels you want. You would find your father not lacking in generosity." Cromwell knew Mary's weakness. He knew the weaknesses of everyone at court.

Mary twisted a strand of her red-gold hair round and round her finger. "I cannot betray my mother, Master Cromwell," she said quietly. "By signing the oath I shall be publicly agreeing that her marriage to my father was void. I could never do that to her. My dearly beloved mother, God keep her."

Cromwell's notions of loyalty were somewhat loose, but he was none the less touched by this girl's pride. She was worth ten of that black-haired bitch below in the hall, flaunting her new crimson gown which had depleted the privy purse by two hundred marks, pulling the bodice a little too low and attracting the lecherous eyes of Henry's gentlemen. He bowed stiffly to Mary, who was still sitting on the bed, and saying, "So be it, lady. I doubt not but you will come to it anon," turned to take his leave.

Before he knew what was happening, the small grey figure with the streaming red hair had rushed past him and through the unlocked door of the chamber. Cromwell shouted, "My lady, stop!" but Mary did not heed the urgent voice as she sped down the passage to the central staircase which zig-zagged down to the hall.

As she rounded the last bend in the stairs the elegant company came into view. Mary's heart missed a beat as she caught sight of her father, legs astride in characteristic attitude, expounding some pet theory to the Duke of Norfolk, whose round, sallow face regarded him attentively. One huge, royal hand held a silver wine goblet which Henry was using to emphasise a point here and there with the result that the contents slopped messily on to the floor, staining the new polished boards.

Henry was dressed in a gold cloth over-tunic trimmed with sable, under which could be seen the close-fitting doublet of emerald green brocade trimmed with bands of jewelled embroidery. The doublet was slashed to show his white silk shirt beneath. His hose were of white silk and his feet were encased in broad jewelled shoes of green leather. At forty-four Henry was just past the prime of life and showing unmistakable signs of the strain he had undergone during the six years when he had been trying to obtain a divorce from Catherine. The rich gold hair had thinned and was now straighter than before and his reddish beard was streaked with grey. Pouches were forming under the small eyes and his face was becoming prematurely lined. He was running to fat. Despite all this, he was still a fine figure of a man.

As Mary descended the last two steps of the staircase Henry roared with laughter at something Norfolk had said and shook his head vigorously. "No, no, Norfolk, you'll never get me to believe that the firmament does not revolve beyond the seventh planetary circle. You are talking nonsense, my lord." A movement of his head brought the small, still figure at the foot of the stairs into his line of vision and he paused, mouth agape, staring at his daughter. A curious expression flitted across his face compounded of pity, agony, joy and fierce anger. He did not move as Mary hurled herself across the chamber at him and kneeling before him clasped his right leg between trembling hands. She looked up beseechingly at her father whose face, down-turned towards hers, was now dark with annoyance. A small purple vein throbbed on his temple.

"Your grace," begged Mary, "I must speak with you. Father, oh Father, please . . . please . . . I . . . I . . . let me explain . . ." Her voice died on a thin scream as rough hands were laid on her shoulders and she was forcibly pulled away from Henry. Madge Shelton hissed into her ear. "You shall pay for this, my lady. Jesu, but you'll pay!"

Frantically, Mary surveyed the company for a sign of a single friendly face. She felt conspicuous in her faded grey gown with its torn braid, and her hair falling about her shoulders like a serving-wench.

The Queen moved towards Henry's side and stood regarding her silently. Her left thumb rubbed compulsively the spot at the base of her little finger where a large naevus sprouted. There were some who insisted that this was an extra finger and a sign that the Queen was in league with the devil. Mary winced as she saw the pouting mouth break into a slow smile and the dark eyes shrewdly calculating how best to taunt her. The back tooth, which had been plaguing her ever since she came to Hatfield, began to throb violently.

Everyone jumped as a female voice shrieked, "Jesu, a rat! Catch it, my lord, or I swear I shall faint!"

There was a confused scramble during which Madge Shelton shoved Mary towards the staircase. Mary looked over her shoulder to see Jane Seymour lying flat on her back surrounded by several ladies and gentlemen. Henry's voice rose stridently above the rest. "Cromwell! Where the devil is Cromwell? I'll have his hide for this!" But Thomas Cromwell had taken refuge in the chapel which he had reached by means of a secondary staircase. He knew just how long to wait there before venturing out to face Henry. Of course, he would still be blamed for allowing Mary to escape from her chamber, but the royal wrath, much to be feared these days, would have cooled somewhat.

2

Up in the bedchamber Madge Shelton was screaming at Mary. "If I were the King's grace I would kick you out of doors to fend for yourself. Ah, but he'll not do that. He has other plans for you, mistress."

"Other plans?" faltered Mary, thinking of Chapuys' warning that Henry might marry her off to some low-born fellow.

"Aye, mistress,' replied Madge spitefully and untruthfully, "he has said that he will have your head if you do not sign the oath."

"Oh, Jesu!" Terrified, Mary stuffed her hand into her mouth and stared at Madge with round, fear-crazed eyes. Madge smirked with satisfaction and marched out of the bedchamber.

All that night Mary lay on her bed conjuring up fearful pictures of herself in the Tower, on trial for treason at Westminster Hall, being led out to the scaffold on Tower Green, the red-clad figure of the headsman begging her pardon for the doleful office he must perform, she kneeling before the block and laying her neck across the narrow, curved bridge, the whirr of the axe as the headsman brought it up high over his head, the hiss as it descended and the grinding crunch . . .

Mary screamed on a high wail of utter despair and terror. Her muddled thoughts had lulled her into a half doze and she was dreaming, just dreaming of the scaffold on Tower Green. No one heard her. No one came to comfort her, but at Kimbolton Castle, half roused by an indefinable sense of something amiss, Catherine of Aragon murmured "Mary" and fell back into a troubled sleep.

The next morning Jane Seymour came to see Mary. Henry had issued no orders to the effect that any of his party were to avoid Mary, but it had been tacitly understood that he would prefer her to be left alone. Bravely Jane ignored the unwritten law. All the same, as she made her way to Mary's chamber after Mass, she was accompanied by Madge Shelton and the Lady Alice Clere, who stuck to her like limpets.

Mary was unashamedly glad to see her and Jane's eyes filled with tears as she sat beside the small defiant figure on the bed who began very politely to inquire after her health. Jane's natural impulse was to take Mary in her arms and hold her close, to stroke away the sad, sad lines of that childish,yet over-mature face. She did not make the gesture. Better she thought to let Mary retain what vestiges of pride she had left.

Mary was asking her something and Jane gathered her wandering thoughts. "Are you learned in Latin, my lady?"

"I speak it fair, though I fear I was not a very apt pupil," replied Jane smiling.

"I have no books to read now," said Mary, "and my tutor has been sent away. Would you mind if I spoke to you in Latin a little so that I may see if I am still conversant with the tongue?"

Madge Shelton frowned suspiciously and said sourly, "You will talk in English, my lady. I want none of your sly tricks."

Jane Seymour rose and advancing on the surprised Madge extended one long white forefinger and poked her painfully in the stomach. Her small, thin mouth was pursed with anger. "If the princess wishes to converse in Latin then let it be so," she said, carefully emphasising each word with several quite vicious stabs. "I would not push matters too far, were I you."

Something in the tone of Jane's voice made Madge take pause and muttering, "So be it then," she went to sit near the window, but she kept her hard blue eyes fixed on Mary and Jane. Lady Clere stood by the door biting her finger-nails and frowning. She was not terribly quick-witted and generally left Madge to do any talking that was necessary.

"Now, your grace," said Jane brightly. "Let us begin. Try me, though I must warn you again, I am no scholar."

Mary did not return Jane's smile, but fixed her instead with a very intent stare which the other found disconcerting. She was about to put into operation a plan which had half-formed itself in her mind during the night, but which she had seen no possibility of putting into action until Jane, dear God-sent Jane, had arrived to see her. "I have been informed," she began, "that my father plans to have me beheaded. I beg that you will tell the Spanish ambassador, Messire Chapuys, so that he may advise me."

Jane almost fainted in earnest this time. What colour there was in her wax-pale cheeks disappeared altogether and she saw black spots before her eyes. Rallying herself sharply, for she could see from the girl's stricken face that her need was urgent, she said as cheerfully as she could so that the two watching women would suspect nothing, "I will tell him, but I think your fears be quite unfounded. Someone is trying to frighten you." She dare not mention any names. "Did someone here in this chamber tell you that tale?"

"Yes."

"The younger lady?"

"Yes."

"Ah! I thought so. I for one do not believe it," and then, as she saw Mary's hands fluttering agitatedly, "Fear not, your grace, I will do as you ask."

Then she was gone, feeling almost as fearful as Mary, but she managed to get a message out to Chapuys that same night, just before the royal party left Hatfield.

3

Jane's message bore fruit. Chapuys began a secret, dangerous correspondence with Mary, but it served its purpose for he succeeded in calming her fears and in convincing her that Madge had spoken without knowledge.

The year 1535 was a dreadful one. Mary moved from Hatfield to Greenwich and from Greenwich to Eltham with the Princess Elizabeth's household and the talk was of Bishop Fisher and Thomas More and the brave Charterhouse monks who had all been butchered on the scaffold. Mary's dream about the headsman and the axe became a recurrent one and it was quite a commonplace now for her to wake screaming in the night. Her tooth began to ache with increasing frequency and she longed to have it pulled but feared to ask for the services of a physician. She heard rumours. She was to be married to the Dauphin of France. Her mother was ill but had recovered and was cooking all her food over a pot in her bedchamber. The Queen was *enciente* again.

Mary was ill herself at Christmas and was surprised when one of her father's own physicians came to attend her. He treated her kindly, cured her rheum and pulled her rotten tooth. Mary fainted during the process, but, oh the blessed relief when it was gone!

Immediately after Christmas Mary sensed a change in the atmosphere. Madge Shelton abruptly ceased her bullying, the Dukes of Norfolk and Suffolk paid her a courtesy visit and conveyed a verbal message from the Queen to the effect that if Mary came to court she would be well received, providing, of course, that the King was not in residence. Her father, said Suffolk, would not see her until she signed the oath. Mary was puzzled by all this and, mull over it though she might, she could find no answer to account for the sudden, friendlier attitude towards her.

Then Thomas Cromwell came to see her. It was the eighth day of January in the new year of 1536 and very cold. A biting wind seemed to find its way through every nook and cranny of the draughty old manor house at Eltham. Mary, wrapped in a fur rug, was playing with Elizabeth in the nursery. She had grown very fond of her half-sister. Her generous heart would never allow her to blame the child for her mother. To Mary, Elizabeth was, like herself, merely the victim of circumstances. The little princess was now a chubby two-and-a-half-year-old with a mind of her own. "Mare, Mare," she demanded shrilly, "give Bess ball."

Smiling, Mary threw a red velvet ball stuffed with goose feathers at the child and roared with laughter as it caught her in her fat little stomach and bowled her over, so that her plump legs waved in the air. Mary was still laughing when Cromwell walked in.

Seeing who it was who had disturbed her brief half-hour of pleasure Mary sighed. Doubtless Master Cromwell had come about the oath again. Cromwell was now Henry's Vicar-General, his task being to see that all churches throughout England and Wales were comforming in the matter of the King's Supremacy.

Before Cromwell could open his mouth Mary shrugged off the fur rug, straightened her shoulders, and burst out, "I will not take the oath, Master Cromwell. I will not. So pray do not tire me with your ceaseless persuasions."

Cromwell did not answer and Mary looked sharply at him. His small brown eyes held a hint of something she had not discerned in them before. Was it? Could it possibly be pity? The old familiar knot of fear cramped Mary's stomach muscles. "You have not come about the oath," she said positively. He shook his head.

"What then? I . . . is it my m . . . mother? Is she ill again?"

Cromwell bowed his head and with eyes fixed to the floor said quietly, "Your lady mother died on Friday, my lady. She is to be buried at Peterborough Abbey on the twenty-sixth day of this present month."

This time the frequent, ready tears failed to come to Mary's aid. She just stood there, staring at Cromwell. Staring and not wanting to believe this terrible truth.

Abruptly, Cromwell turned and left the nursery, returning within a minute or two with a girl of about Mary's own age who held in her hands some furs and a gold cross on a chain.

"Your lady mother left you these in her will," Cromwell told Mary, indicating the items which the girl now held out towards her, "and may I present to you Mistress Jane Dormer, who is to be your lady-in-waiting."

"My lady-in-waiting?" queried Mary with dull surprise.

"The King thinks 'tis time you had a lady-in-waiting," said Cromwell non-committally.

"Oh." Mary's voice was blank. This was another small instance of the subtle changes which had been taking place recently.

Jane Dormer, a sturdy girl with peach-bloom cheeks and glossy black hair, which escaped rebelliously from the confines of her hood, stepped forward and curtsied to Mary. Mary looked into the large, sympathetic hazel eyes and now the tears for her mother flowed freely.

"Ah there, my lady, don't, don't," said Jane, and folding Mary in her arms, crooned gently to her in her broad country accents, treating her just as she would any love-sick or distressed dairy-maid on her father's manor at Bishop's Cleeve in Gloucestershire.

Soon Mary ceased to sob and taking her mother's cross from Jane placed it reverently about her neck. Jane smiled and nodded at her and Cromwell left them together. Elizabeth, who had watched the scene with interest, picked up her velvet ball and threw it at Jane.

4

They were going to bury her mother at Peterborough when she had specifically requested in her will that she be laid to rest in a convent of Observant Friars, and the court was donning yellow satin and rejoicing at her death. Lady Bryan had received orders to dress the little Elizabeth in yellow satin and bring her to Greenwich for the festivities. Under the bright, rich material the princess still wore diapers. Shocked, Mary watched Lady Bryan dressing the princess. "Surely they have all run mad," she said.

Lady Bryan shrugged bewilderedly. " 'Tis by order of the King." He *is* bewitched, thought Mary. I must believe that, else will I run mad too.

She did not know it yet, but the enchantment was wearing off. On the same day that Catherine was buried, Queen Anne miscarried of a boy child and the last slender thread which bound her to Henry was broken. For long, unknown to Mary, her father had been tired of his gaudy wife, and in failing to bear him a son she had done the one thing for which he could never forgive her. In May, 1536, therefore she was arrested on a trumped-up charge of adultery, arraigned before twenty-six peers in the great hall at the Tower, found guilty and sentenced to death. She was executed on Tower Green on May 19 wearing a red damask gown and hoping to the last for a reprieve. None came.

After her execution Mary received a message from Chapuys that he was coming to Eltham and would she meet him in the chapel at midnight. Mary smiled as she read the scribbled note. How like Chapuys to suggest midnight for a meeting when she could just as easily, if a trifle riskily, have slipped out of her bedchamber at nine of the clock when the household was abed.

She went to the chapel just before midnight. Chapuys was already there, crouched before the altar. She sat down beside him and waited expectantly. He moved a little closer to her and she could feel his breath on her neck. "I have come," he began, "because I fear the King's grace may soon press you again to take the Oath of Succession."

"Has he said so?"

"Yes, and he grows impatient. Methinks that this time he will brook no refusal."

"And if I do refuse?"

Mary could not see the expression on Chapuys' face, which was only a pale blur in the moonlit chapel, but his voice shook slightly as he said, "I would tremble for your safety, my princess."

Mary said shrewdly, "Yes, he has killed one woman who was close to him, so it is quite possible he will not hesitate to kill a second."

"That could be so."

"What am I to do?"

She spoke quite calmly and Chapuys looked at her curiously. "The idea of death does not strike terror to your heart as it once did?"

"No . . . o . . . o," said Mary slowly. "Since my mother's death my faith in God has grown stronger. I find now that I can accept His will in all things, even to the uttermost."

"Your highness must not talk of acceptance." Chapuys, though a devout enough Catholic, was practical. "Here is what you must do," he said. "If the commissioners come to you again you will sign the oath and . . ." Mary opened her mouth to protest but Chapuys stayed her with a gesture of his hand, ". . . and I shall give you a form of protest to sign which I will send to the Emperor. That will nullify your having signed the oath and your father will be none the wiser."

Mary was doubtful. "I shall still have betrayed my mother."

"No, no, highness, that you will not. God judges only the intention, not the act."

But Mary's mind still refused to consider the possibility of signing the oath so she changed the subject. "Did the Lady Anne die well?" she asked, hating herself for the question, which she knew stemmed only from morbid curiosity.

"Yes," admitted Chapuys, momentarily side-tracked. "She spoke briefly to the people gathered about the scaffold and she submitted herself to the headsman with dignity . . . Yes, with dignity. I am bound to say so, though I liked her not at all." Chapuys was a fair man for all his violent partisanship of Mary.

Mary shuddered. She had thought that at worst Henry would have banished Anne to a convent. The mental picture she formed of that slender white neck being severed by the sword of the Calais executioner turned her stomach. "Poor strange lady," she murmured, finding to her intense surprise that all her vengeful feelings had disappeared now that Anne was dead and the little Elizabeth doomed to become a bastard like herself.

"And what of all those young men who died with her?" she went on, "Norrys, Weston, Brereton, George Boleyn and Mark Smeaton, her musician." Mary ticked the names off on her fingers and looked at Chapuys almost pleadingly. "She must have been guilty Messire. Father would not have killed an innocent woman. She must have committed adultery with at least one of them."

Chapuys shrugged. "Who knows? Myself I am inclined to think that she was too afraid of the King ever to have taken such a risk, but, of course, there was the question of the heir."

Mary's eyes opened wide. "You mean she could have . . . er, she could have . . . to get an heir? Pass off a bastard as heir to the throne?"

"Who would know the difference?"

"If she committed adultery with anyone I'll wager it was with that Mark Smeaton," declared Mary. "I liked him not at all, what little I saw of him."

" 'Tis true he *said* she lay with him, but that was under torture and that one would not stand up long under the rack."

Mary stretched and yawned, feeling a sudden reluctance to continue this conversation about the dead Queen. " 'Tis fruitless to speculate," she said. "We shall never get at the truth of the matter." She yawned again. "And so father is to marry again. I can scarce believe that Mistress Jane Seymour is to be his new bride."

"She does not want to marry the King's grace," replied Chapuys emphatically. "She is being forced to it by those brothers of hers. Ambitious young men, the Seymours. They were quick to take advantage of the fact that the King expressed admiration for Mistress Seymour's forthright honesty and the way she was not afraid to speak well of your highness."

"I shall never forget her kindness to me," said Mary warmly. "She has a brave heart. I cannot think how it was that I did not hear rumours of father's attachment for her."

"The King kept the matter close," answered Chapuys. "He told only a few of his counsellors."

"How . . . er, how long have they . . . er, have they . . .?"

Chapuys helped her out. "About a year."

So Jane could not have known anything when she came to Hatfield that time, thought Mary, yet was she kind to me just the same. Aloud she said, "The Lady Jane likes me enough to intercede with father for me. Perhaps she can persuade him that I need not sign the oath and then I can go to court and . . ."

Chapuys was shaking his head vigorously and Mary stopped short. "The lady will not be able to influence the King in so important a matter," he told her.

Mary said with sudden vehemence, "That cursed oath, it *will* be the death of me in the end." She realised that she was not so resigned to death as she had imagined and once more fear took possession of her. "Oh Jesu, sweet Jesu," she moaned. "What am I to do? What am I to do?"

To her surprise she felt Chapuys' arm circle her shoulders and then his mouth was on her cheek. Her legs felt weak and she experienced an unfamiliar, tingling lassitude in her thighs. Blindly she offered her mouth to Chapuys. His instinct was to kiss her passionately and press her body close to his, for he was not a little in love with her. Wisely he resisted the dictates of his heart. He kissed her gently, like a brother, offering her the affection she craved and as she sighed contentedly he whispered, "Put your trust in Spain, higness. Trust the Emperor. He will see that no harm befalls you."

From that day forth the Spanish half of Mary began to assert itself.

HUNSDON–GREENWICH–HAMPTON COURT

July, 1536–October, 1537

I

In the end she was forced to sign the oath. She was to hate herself ever afterwards for what she considered to be a cowardly and treacherous act and at night she would weep until her head ached beyond bearing. At first she had tried to obtain audience with her father through the medium of Thomas Cromwell. She wrote him letter after letter explaining, begging, pleading and always the replies were the same. "If you will sign the oath. If you will but sign the oath. Submit. Sign the oath. Submit. Sign the oath." The words reverberated in her head until they seemed like some strange witch's incantation to be repeated over and over to ward off evil spirits.

She was now at Hunsdon, still part of the household of the Princess Elizabeth, and Chapuys came there often to see her, adding his voice to Cromwell's now in an urgent plea for her to sign, sign, sign. He knew, none better, the temper of the King's moods and with that knowledge came the realisation that Henry, the gay Tudor, had turned into a dangerous, treacherous beast. Yes, there was danger in the air. Chapuys could smell it with his long Savoyard nose. Mary must be made to sign the oath. So Chapuys argued and cajoled, produced his well-worded protest, told her he would obtain for her immediate absolution from the Pope and at last, at last she agreed. Chapuys heaved a heartfelt sigh of relief, hurried back to court and informed Thomas Cromwell breathlessly that the princess was prepared to submit. At once Cromwell told the King, and commissioners were sent that same afternoon to Hunsdon with the necessary papers.

Mary received them in the small ante-chamber adjoining the hall and there was not a man among them who, gazing on the small, insignificant figure before them, did not marvel that so poor a creature could have defied their magnificent King for so long. She regarded them gravely, her hands folded neatly before her. Suffolk, Norfolk, Lord Chancellor Audley, Thomas Wriothesley, lately come to favour and

Edward Seymour, Viscount Beauchamp, Jane Seymour's brother. Mary looked at the latter curiously. He did not resemble Jane in the least this tall, thin young man with the huge, deep-set brown eyes, long nose and receding chin from which sprouted an unfashionably long, mousy-brown beard. He did not look ambitious, but then one could never tell where ambition lurked.

Norfolk greeted her curtly, his sallow face, round as a silver penny, unsmiling. "So, lady, you have come to your senses at last. God's bones, but if I had been your father I'd not have had his grace's patience. I'd have knocked your silly head against a stone wall until it was soft as a baked apple."

He signed impatiently to Audley to lay out the papers on the table which Lady Shelton had already furnished with inkstand, quills and wax for the sealing.

Mary was used to bullying. She was now almost immune to it. "I wish to take the papers to my chamber that I may read them carefully and alone," she said in her clear voice which was beginning to take on a distinctly masculine tone, "then will I sign them and bring them to your lordships if you will please to wait here."

Before the astonished commissioners could reply Mary swept up the papers, together with the inkstand and a quill and had disappeared through the door. At least, she thought grimly as she mounted the stairs to her chamber, I shall deny them the pleasure of actually *seeing* me sign.

Norfolk found his voice first and fairly howled after her, "Come back here, you brat! Come back, I say. Lady Shelton! Lady Shelton! God's nails, but someone will smoke for this!" Lady Shelton came on the run and was despatched to Mary's bedchamber to prise her out. She found the door barred from within and despite frantic appeals, followed by the inevitable threats, received for answer only an implacable silence. She returned, sour-faced to Norfolk to report the failure of her mission.

2

Mary kept the impatient commissioners waiting for three hours while she knelt before her *prie-dieu* and begged forgiveness for the great sin she was about to commit. The jewelled figure of the Virgin, in her niche above the *prie-dieu*, glowed in the light of the red sanctuary lamp and gave her comfort. When, exhausted, she rose at last from her knees, she calmly appended her signature to every page of Audley's document without bothering to read the contents. She knew only too well the gist of the three clauses at which she had baulked for so long—". . . I hereby acknowledge Henry VIII, King of England, to be Supreme Head of the Church in England; . . . I hereby declare that it is my opinion that King Henry's marriage to Queen Catherine of Aragon was null and void by virtue of the fact that it was made incestuously; . . . I hereby declare myself to be a bastard."

Mary felt completely devoid of feeling as she descended the stairs to the ante-chamber, the papers in her hand, and coolly presented them to the Lord Chancellor. Fat little Audley bowed awkwardly as he accepted them. Without casting so much as a single glance in the direction of the other men Mary turned her back on them and quitted the chamber, leaving Audley to affix the ribbons and seals. She had no seal of her own so presumably Audley would affix his. She did not care. Nothing mattered any more. She had betrayed her dead mother. Sunk to the very depths. She was completely drained of feeling. But when she reached the privacy of her chamber a grey cloud of misery such as she had never before known descended on her and she fell to the floor, clenching her fists in an agony of remorse. She lay as one dead until a merciful blackness enveloped her.

When Chapuys came to see her the next day she met him, dry-eyed and strangely composed. "I have betrayed my God and my mother," she told him almost matter-of-factly. "Now 'tis done and cannot be undone. But I swear by the Blessed Virgin that henceforth I shall do only what I believe to be right, whatever the cost." Her voice rose slightly, "Whatever the cost, Messire Chapuys. Never again will I resort to cowardly compromise such as this." She thrust at him a copy of the signed protest he had drawn up for her. "Here, take it. Take it."

"That copy is for your grace," answered Chapuys awkwardly. "The original has already been despatched to the Emperor. That one you must keep privily locked in your coffer."

"Take it!" shrilled Mary. "I do not want the cursed thing about my chamber."

In the angry grey eyes Chapuys saw the first hint of a fanaticism which was to become more and more apparent as the years passed, and he trembled for her.

3

Three weeks went by before Mary received the much-desired summons to come to court and when it arrived she was not so elated as she had expected to be. Now that her long struggle was over, the reward for her betrayal seemed trifling indeed. All the same it would mean that she would now have her freedom after eight years of virtual imprisonment. Cromwell had hinted in a letter to her that the King was talking of re-establishing her household which would mean that she would no longer have to serve Elizabeth. And too, Chapuys had obtained for her, in secret, of course, the Pope's absolution for signing the Oath of Succession, contained in a clearly worded Bull. This had been a great consolation to Mary and as Chapuys had pointed out, her mother was with God, so that nothing she could do here on earth could possibly harm her, and in the end, when the secrets of all hearts were known . . . Thus did Mary console herself as she prepared for the journey to court.

After three years Greenwich looked much as she had remembered it, but she was startled as she entered the great hall to look up at the painted pendants and see thereon the initials 'H' and 'A' entwined where once had been 'H' and 'C'. It was odd, after everything she had been made to suffer, that this should give her the biggest shock of all.

Even as she stood there, with Jane Dormer close at her side, some workmen were bringing in trestles, long ladders and pots of gilded paint. "They are going to paint out the 'A's' now," said Mary wonderingly to Jane. She experienced a made desire to laugh, the sort of laughter that could so easily dissolve into screaming hysterics. She choked it back firmly, still gazing about her. She felt lonely, standing there with only Jane beside her, for the rest of the few household servants who had accompanied them were busy seeing to the accommodation. Mary hoped it would be better than the last time she had come to Greenwich!

A page was bawling Henry's titles and the door at the far end of the hall behind the dais was thrown open. Mary just had time to think that so much formality was a little unnecessary considering that she and Jane and a handful of workmen were the only occupants of the hall, before Henry, his new Queen walking beside him, was advancing towards her, followed by the usual bevy of ladies and gentlemen.

Mary's knees turned to water as she sank into a deep curtsy and she could sense that Jane Dormer, who was unused to the ways of the court, was in an agony of embarrassment. This fact immediately gave her courage and to her surprise she found herself presenting Jane to Henry quite naturally. The King had not previously met the girl, having left the choosing of her to Thomas Cromwell.

Henry greeted his daughter with a sort of forced joviality which she found almost harder to bear than his previous sour displeasure. He raised her to her feet and drawing her towards him kissed her on the mouth, but the old warmth of her childhood days had gone and she felt as if this were some polite and distant relative saluting her, one whom she had not seen for many years. Mary noticed that her father had grown much stouter since that dreadful day at Hatfield. Above the jewelled belt his blue doublet bulged alarmingly and his shoulders, under the gold velvet over-tunic, looked enormous. Her cheeks burned with embarrassment for Henry just stood there staring at her with a blank expression on his face, an expression impossible to interpret because it conveyed absolutely nothing.

The Queen saved the awkward situation by embracing Mary warmly and slipping on to her finger a diamond ring of great value. Mary gasped with pleasure. It was the first gift of any worth she had received for several years.

"Y . . . your grace, much thanks," she said shyly, feeling a little strange at having to address Jane thus. "You are too kind."

Jane smiled broadly, her pale, homely face expressing the intense pleasure she felt at this reunion between father and daughter. "The King has something for you that I warrant you will like even better," she said and looked at Henry expectantly.

"Ah yes, yes, so I have," said Henry, coming out of his trance. "Bring it here, Cromwell."

Thomas Cromwell broke away from the group of gentlemen with whom he had been standing and producing a purse of read leather from the sleeve of his tunic presented it to Henry who, in turn, proffered it to Mary. "That should buy you a few new gowns, daughter," he said with something like his old cheerful manner. "You will find within two thousand crowns to spend at your pleasure."

Mary was rendered speechless. Even in the old days before her disgrace she had never possessed so much all at one time.

She thought of all the things she could buy with it. New gowns, gloves, a new palfrey maybe and she would not forget her dear friend Jane Dormer who needed a gown almost as badly as she did herself. In the few months they had been together Mary and Jane had become very close.

Cromwell's quiet voice cut across her thoughts. "My lady, I, too, have a gift for you, if it will please you to accept it." He held out a gold medallion set with rubies and emeralds and hanging from a gold chain.

A little taken aback, for it was not usual for a commoner, however exalted, to present a member of the King's family with a gift of jewellery, Mary examined the medallion closely. On the front, in high relief, were profile portraits of her father and Jane, and on the reverse the words, "God loves a humble heart," had been inscribed in Latin. Before she could stop it the thought flashed through her mind, "I wonder if God loves a traitor," but she quelled it before it had time to take root and trouble her. She wanted nothing to spoil this most auspicious day. She smiled up at Thomas Cromwell and murmured her thanks. "I shall wear it about my neck," she said. The fat, double-chinned face with the thick, blunt features smiled back at her and he bowed in token of his gratification of her acceptance of his gift. Henry said casually, "Master Cromwell has a great affection for you, Mary. He went to a deal of trouble to have his gift made for you. It is the work of Master Wollesey of Cheapside, the finest goldsmith in London."

"It was kind indeed of Master Cromwell," said Mary dutifully. She thought that Cromwell must be very high in Henry's favour for the King to commend him with such fervour. She was still looking at the medallion, turning it over and over in her fingers, and she did not notice the speculative glance the Queen gave Henry, but others did and wondered, like Jane, whether Henry could really be contemplating marrying off his troublesome daughter to Thomas Cromwell.

4

As Cromwell had predicted, Mary's household was to be re-established, and it was arranged that she should stay at Greenwich while this was being carried out. It was decided that she should reside at Hunsdon and that the Princess Elizabeth should be removed to Hatfield with a separate establishment. Mary learned with joy that Susan Clarencieux and Mary Browne, who had both joined her household at the time she had been made Princess of Wales, were to be returned to her, but when they offered her Margaret Douglas, now married to Matthew Stuart, Earl of Lennox, she rather tactlessly declined the services of that lady. She did not care if she gave offence to Margaret. She had had enough of sharp-tongued women.

She returned to Hunsdon just before Christmas of the year 1536 and took her leave of Elizabeth. The child, now three, stood in the inner hall at Hunsdon, wrapped in polecat furs, her pale, freckled face serious and unsmiling. She was sorry to be going away from Mary, with whom she had played such jolly games. Her small hand held up a rather grubby looking object which she offered proudly to Mary. "For you, sister," she said, "Bess made it."

Mary sank to her knees and drawing the child towards her took the badly stitched purse which Elizabeth had made for her as a parting gift. A very crooked 'M' surmounted by a coronet had been embroidered on one side of a drawstring purse fashioned out of white velvet, a somewhat unfortunate choice of material for a boisterous child. It was, none the less, a very worthy effort for a three-year-old.

Touched beyond measure, Mary's eyes filled with the tears which were never far from the surface. She hugged Elizabeth to her and thanked her a thousand times for her lovely, lovely gift with which she would never, never part. Impulsively she took from her finger a ruby ring which had once belonged to her grandmother, Elizabeth of York and gave it to Elizabeth.

Lady Bryan, muffled to the ears in a blue felt cloak against the bitter winter weather, instantly protested. "The gift is too rich, your grace. The child will lose it. Can you not find something more fitting? A kerchief perhaps?"

But Elizabeth, who was already showing signs of the acquisitiveness which was to become one of her least likeable characteristics, had tied the ring to a ribbon decorating her gown, it being too large for her small fingers, and was now frowning up at Lady Bryan so incredibly fiercely that both women could not forbear to laugh.

"Let the child keep it," said Mary complacently. "I misdoubt me very much if she will lose it. See, she has it safe secured to her person." Mary could not help being reminded of her grandfather, King Henry the Seventh, whose mania for collecting money and jewels had almost surpassed the bounds of decency. Obviously Elizabeth took after him. Smiling she kissed Elizabeth again and after seeing her comfortably bestowed in her litter with Lady Bryan beside her she waved her on her way to Hatfield.

5

Mary went to court for the Christmas festivities and managed to enter into the spirit of rejoicing quite successfully but the celebrations were spoiled for her somewhat because Henry developed a habit of forcing her into converse and immediately broaching the subject of her final submission to him. Backing her up against a wall he would bar escape with his huge torso and invariably he would begin the conversation with the words, "Tell me now, daughter, were you really sincere when you signed the oath? Was it done with a truly humble heart?"

And then, "Do you think of me as Supreme Head of the Church in England? Do you think of yourself as a bastard?" This last question was always accompanied by a thrusting forward of the royal chin and an insulting emphasis on the final word. Then, one day, apparently apropos of nothing, he demanded abruptly, "How would you like to marry Thomas Cromwell?"

Mary's cheeks paled and she stammered, "I . . . I . . . er, I . . . do not know. I am not on familiar terms with Master Cromwell, that is to say I . . ." Mary floundered helplessly.

"Think yourself too good for him, eh? Eh?"

Desperately Mary sought for a way out. She wanted to shout at her father, "Yes, yes, yes! I am too good for him. I am your daughter and the daughter of a princess of Spain. Yes, God rot you, I am too good for the son of a blacksmith!" But she dared not speak her mind. She wished heartily that Jane were pregnant because she knew she would never be safe until Henry had the long-desired male heir. So she swallowed her pride, bowed her head, and said submissively enough, though the words bade fair to choke her, "No, Father, I do not think that. If it be your wish I will marry Thomas Cromwell."

He had let her go then and she had counted rapidly on her fingers. Four more days before she could get back to Hunsdon. Once there she hoped her father would perhaps forget about his outrageous idea of marrying her to Cromwell. Perhaps Jane would get with child. Oh Blessed Virgin, let her get with child, she prayed.

The day before she was due to leave court Mary returned to the great hall after supper, having mislaid her kerchief. She found it under the board where she had been sitting and nodding in friendly fashion to the serving-maids who were removing the goblets, she was about to leave the hall when she spied Thomas Cromwell standing in the passage beyond the main door. Wildly Mary looked about her. There was only one other way she could get out and that was through the covered way to the kitchens and so into the courtyard. Either that or she could take refuge in the musicians' gallery. She chose the former course and caused a great deal of shocked surprise in the kitchens as she sped past the long tables piled high with left-over food, stumbled over the spit boy who had fallen asleep by the hearth and kicked one of the cats into a yowling, hissing bundle of ginger fur.

Speculation ran high in the kitchens. Was the Lady Mary going to meet a lover? Was she running away? Had she gone crazed in the head? Any one of these possibilities seemed likely when you thought of the way the poor lady had been treated. Mary realised the stir she was causing but she did not care. Anything was better than meeting Thomas Cromwell face to face. He must know that her father had mentioned the subject of marriage to her and knowing, might be waiting for an opportunity to make her a formal proposal.

She raced across the courtyard and up the outside staircase to the long gallery. Pushing open the door she closed it behind her and leaned against it for a moment, expelling a long sigh of relief. She was just about to commence the long walk to the further end when an arm shot out, apparently from nowhere, and caught her round the waist.

Thomas Cromwell, who had witnessed her precipitate 'escape' from the hall and had guessed accurately which way she would re-enter the palace, had been waiting for her, discreetly hidden in a window recess. Mary struggled free from the encircling arm and turned to face him. "Master Cromwell," she said indignantly, trying to sound authoritative, "you forget yourself. Take care I do not report your unseemly conduct to my father."

"Who would be mighty pleased I'll wager," said Cromwell, smiling his gentle smile, and moving a little closer towards her. Mary backed away. Relentlessly Cromwell pursued her and now there was nothing left of the fatherly attitude which had hitherto characterised his conduct towards her. Now he was the hunter in pursuit of his quarry.

At twenty-one Mary was almost entirely innocent of the ways of men in love or just plain lustful. She began to be frightened. She could not imagine what this man could do to actually harm her, but she knew that there was something a man did to a woman, concerned with his privy parts, which was only permitted after they were married and which invariably resulted in the painful bearing of children. She knew too that adultery meant doing that same thing with someone who was not your husband. "M . . . Master Cromwell, I shall shout for help," she threatened.

"They'll not hear you, lady," answered Cromwell confidently. "They are all drunk as watermen after their supper wine and in bed most like with their wives and lemans." This last was said with a sly sort of leer which frightened Mary even more. Over a hundred candles illuminated the long gallery. They would not be snuffed until after midnight, it being Christmas. By their flickering yellow light Cromwell's face looked distinctly sinister. He tired suddenly of Mary's reluctance. After what she had been through the girl should be glad to have him as her protector. She could expect no better match and once she was married to him she would never have to worry again. She would be safe from her father's wrath for ever. He felt sorry for her, but the King had said he could have her and that was that. He made a lunge for her and again caught her about the waist. With his left arm he pulled her to him and his right hand fumbled at the neck of her gown. His long nails dug into the immature swell of her left breast and he whispered foul obscenities at her, spewing forth words which she had never before heard, in the hope that they would rouse her.

Mary's eyes were glazed with terror. She screamed once, then, in a last desperate effort, brought up her right leg and kicked out at Cromwell as hard as she could. The toe of her leather shoe caught him fair and square in the abdomen. Cursing, he released her and clutched his belly. Mary did not wait to see what damage she had done. She sped down the gallery, grabbing at her disarranged hood. Cromwell called after her, "Who do you think you are, lady? You rotten little bastard, I'll . . ."

Mary did not hear what he would do, for she was already within the sanctuary of her bedchamber, pouring out her heart to her shocked ladies.

6

Early in the New Year of 1537 Mary heard with heartfelt gratitude that Jane was *enceinte*. In her relief she sent the Queen, now at Hampton Court, numerous presents, both practical and impractical. Jane acknowledged them with kind little notes expressing her pleasure. As the months passed and Cromwell did not visit Hunsdon Mary's fears began to lessen. She had sworn her ladies to secrecy over the affair of his assault upon her person and she trusted them implicitly not to divulge to anyone details of the unfortunate, distasteful episode. She received no word from Henry on the subject and indeed he had had second thoughts soon after she left court. His ministers had strongly advised him against making such a match for his daughter. The Emperor, whose alliance was badly needed, would possibly go so far as to declare war on England if he got wind of such a move to dispose of Mary. Henry knew they spoke truth and when Jane told him she was with child he discarded the idea altogether.

Early in October Mary went to court to be present at the birth. There she had a happy reunion with Elizabeth who was very proud of the fact that she was to carry the chrysom at the child's christening. Every day she plagued Mary to rehearse her in her part and Mary good-naturedly obliged, but when she went to see Jane she found her oddly despondent and quite disinterested in the coming event. Her ladies told Mary privately that the Queen refused to look at anything that had been prepared for the baby, including the elaborately trimmed cradle, and indeed when Mary presented her with some beautifully worked smocks which she had made herself Jane merely thanked her politely and placing them on her bed sighed deeply. Mary was puzzled and not a little alarmed by Jane's peculiar attitude and wondered whether it signified a stillbirth. Her poor mother had experienced so many stillbirths. They were quite a commonplace amongst high-born ladies. Every day Mary lit candles for Jane in the palace chapel and twice she made a special intention to which she adhered faithfully. She had been at Hampton Court a week before Jane's pains began and as soon as the Queen's ladies informed her that she was in labour Mary went to her chamber and sitting by the bed held her hand. She did not leave her side until, fourteen hours later, the Queen, almost dead with fatigue and pain, was delivered of a prince.

The King, who had stayed this time to be near his wife, was immediately informed and came on the run. He was in a positive transport of joy. Mary took the newly-washed babe from the hands of the midwife and held him out to her father, who took the child reverently and held him to his breast. "My son," he breathed. "My own son!"

Bossily the midwife took the child from his father and Henry did not protest. A great peace had descended upon him and he was in love with all the world. He looked at Mary who was bending over Jane solicitously and administering a heavy sleeping draught. "A son, Mary," he said. "I have a son."

Mary smiled up at him and even Jane managed a weak parting of her white lips before her eyelids drooped and she fell into a deep sleep.

All that day and the next Henry moved about in a daze. He declared that his son should be named Edward because he was born on the eve of the translation of the Blessed St. Edward. It seemed as though all the troubled years had passed from him and he had returned to the gay, laughing Tudor of the old days. It seemed so, but it was not so, for when Mary, confident that her boon would be granted, asked that Jane might be excused attendance at the christening ceremony because she was still so very weak and feverish, Henry had frowned and answered, "Certainly not. The prince's mother must be there. 'Tis only fitting."

Saddened, Mary turned away, for she too had thought that some miraculous change had been wrought in Henry. So Jane was carried to the chapel at Hampton Court on a velvet-draped couch and was forced to lie throughout the four-hour long service with icy draughts lifting the lappet of her hood and freezing her feet. Her fever heightened and she was already falling into delirium when they carried her back to her apartments. Ten days later she was dead of puerperal fever and rejoicing turned to mourning. This time the court wore purple. Mary kept the all-night vigil beside Jane's body with the other ladies. She, too, had caught cold in the chapel and the eerie night silence was broken by her constant snufflings as she applied her kerchief to her nose. As she tried to concentrate on the prayers for the dead a face kept imprinting itself behind her closed eyelids, someone she had seen at the christening, half-seen and wondered about. A man. Who had it been? He had carried Elizabeth at one point in the proceedings. Suddenly it came to her. Of course! The King had made Thomas Boleyn, Earl of Wiltshire, father to the dead Queen Anne, walk in the procession. No, Henry had not changed.

GREENWICH

October, 1545

I

Listlessly, Mary sat watching her ladies packing her travelling chests for the second of her thrice-yearly visits to court. Her hand went out for the silver goblet which Jane Dormer had placed on a small table close by her side, and she drank some of the soothing mixture compounded of jasmine flowers, poppy seeds and hippocras. Jesu, this headache was killing her and the potion seemed to be slow in working today. Mary was now twenty-nine years old and ever since her twenty-fifth birthday she had suffered from periodic bouts of amenorrhoea. These were always accompanied by violent headaches and feelings of hysteria which were only relieved by the onset of the period. She was suffering from one such bout now. She wished heartily that she could put off her visit to court, but Henry was sure to suspect that she was 'up to something', the Blessed Virgin knew what, and Edward, poor child, would be sore disappointed. It was quite gratifying to know how he looked forward to her visits. Of course, her father's present wife was a dear, sweet lady and very kind to Edward, but she had not known his mother at all well and Mary had. Edward loved to talk about his mother and would press Mary to recount every little incident in Jane's life which she could remember.

Since Jane's death, eight years before, Edward had had three stepmothers and the realm had bee plunged into a turbulent period of religious disturbance. In 1535 Henry had ordered Cromwell to set about the task of closing down the abbeys which, as Supreme Head of the Church, he considered were merely expensive and luxurious establishments to house idle monks. Abbey lands and abbey possessions fell to the crown and Henry used them to reward those whom he favoured. A mass share-out of confiscated lands and chattels began. The men of Lincolnshire and Yorkshire protested against the desecration of their abbeys, which gave many a poor man food and shelter and lit the bleak countryside on dark winter evenings with a blaze of welcoming light, and marched on London to petition the King. A month later their lifeless bodies could be seen hanging like rotting fruit from the trees in their native villages.

Late in 1539 Cromwell, thinking to preserve the balance of power in Europe, where France and Spain had now formed a strong alliance, found Henry a Lutheran bride from Flanders. Henry did not take to Anne of Cleves. She was too fat, too loud in her speech, too gaudily dressed. Too everything in fact. Cromwell paid for his mistake with his life.

Before this fourth marriage the King, with sudden, unexplained ferocity, had turned on his Plantagenet kin, those who lived to remind him that royalty had not begun with the Tudors. Lord Montague and his brother, sons of Margaret, Countess of Salisbury, were arrested, tried for high treason and executed. So too was Henry Courtenay, Marquis of Exeter, the son of Catherine Plantagenet, Edward the Fourth's youngest daughter. His son, Edward, a mere boy was held prisoner in the Tower. After that there had been almost no one left to persecute. Almost. But the old Countess of Salisbury, now nearly seventy, still lived on in her manor house at Wimborne. Henry dragged her out of retirement on a ridiculous charge of being in possession of a banner embroidered with the arms of Pole impaled with the royal arms of England and sent her to the Tower.

Mary rose from her stool, returning the goblet to the table as she did so, and went to stand by the window. Jane Dormer, Susan Clarencieux and Mary Browne, chattered on as they packed her gowns and hoods, unaware of the sudden violent turmoil taking place in their mistress's breast. Mary opened the window and sucked in great breaths of the sharp autumn air. She still experienced a feeling of nausea, accompanied by dizzying faintness whenever she thought of the countess, who, having been tried and found guilty of high treason, had been condemned to die on the scaffold. She had been held prisoner in the Tower for two years under sentence of death, and then, one bright morning, they had taken her out through the great doorway of the Beauchamp Tower to where the headsman waited for her on Tower Green, an inexperienced headsman, the regular man being busy up north with the remnants of the rebels from Yorkshire whose "pilgrimage of grace" had ended so disastrously. The brave old woman had refused to lay her head on the block when politely, if somewhat nervously, requested to do so. "So should traitors do," she had snapped. "I am none. If you would have my head you must take it if you can." And so the headsman had been forced to chase her round the scaffold, hacking at her with the axe, smattering the watching crowd with pieces of her bloodied flesh until she succumbed at last and fell, a grey, crumpled heap at his feet. Ah God, thy courage aunt, surpasses mine, breathed Mary. Thou wert royal indeed.

Before the execution of the countess the ageing King, having almost slaked his thirst for revenge, had sought a new wife. His eye lighted on another of the Howard brood, a small, plump, red-headed girl of seventeen, Catherine Howard. His rose without a thorn he called her, but the thorns had sprouted one dark night when the little Catherine, sick of the decaying smell of her old husband, lay with her sweet-breathed cousin Thomas Culpepper. They had arrested her while she was dancing a pavane in the hall at Hampton Court. " 'Tis no longer the time to dance," they told her. How frightened she had been, the poor little Howard, escaping from her guards to run screaming down the long gallery to the door of the chapel where Henry was at his devotions. Her headless body lay now, beside that of her cousin, Anne Boleyn, in the chapel of St. Peter ad Vincula hard by the Tower. Now Henry was married to Catherine Parr, twice widowed already, a slender, dark lady with a studious turn of mind and a kind heart. Mary sighed. If only she could have been married with children to love and cherish. Useless to think thus. While her father lived she would be only the Lady Mary, the most unhappy lady in Christendom.

The journey to court, at present lodged at Greenwich, revived Mary's spirits somewhat. She always felt better when she was out in the fresh air. She arrived before supper and discovered her brother Edward in the small closet adjoining Henry's presence chamber which was used as a schoolroom.

Edward was sitting at a table, scribbling furiously on a sheet of parchment. Queen Catherine was with him, seated at the same table and going over some accounts. She rose when the page announced Mary and greeted her warmly. Mary returned the greeting in kind and seeing what she had been about said smilingly, "You should leave your accounts to your Comptroller, Madam. That is what he is paid for."

Catherine's round, pink face with its merry brown eyes smiled back. "Do not tease me, Mary," she reproved. "You know I like fiddling with accounts and these are only my privy purse expenses."

Edward was tugging at Mary's skirt. "Come, Mary, see what I have written," he said eagerly. "'Tis all in Latin. Master Cheke says my Latin is very good for a boy of my age."

Mary looked down at the small, pinched face upturned towards hers. The blue eyes were Jane's, but the rest of the face was all Tudor, from the high, pale forehead, the arrogant nose and the small, pursed mouth. Edward was dressed today in a crimson velvet doublet overlaid with bands of silver braid. His breeches matched his doublet and his hose were of black silk. Red leather shoes, decorated with silver medallions, encased his feet. The costly clothes ill-fitted his spare frame.

Mary bent over Edward's writing. Before she could begin to read, however, he said importantly, "'Tis my journal, Mary. I record in it all the happenings in my life."

"Oh." Mary wondered what Edward could possibly find to write about of the rather dull day to day existence he led, enlivened only by occasional presentations to visiting ambassadors and the usual seasonal festivities. "October 18th, 1545," she read. "Today Barnaby Paycocke taught me a vile word and I repeated it to Master Cheke who gave Barnaby six strokes of the birch." Mary put her fist to her mouth to stop herself laughing. "Poor Barnaby," she murmured.

"Oh, he is not hurt," said Edward carelessly. "He had my Latin grammar stuffed down his breeches." He added primly, "I work very hard and pay attention to my lessons, Mary. Master Cheke hardly ever has to beat *me*."

Mary was suddenly overwhelmed with pity at the mere thought of that thin, slightly pathetic figure being whipped. At that moment Catherine, who had resumed work on her accounts, looked up sharply, rose from her stool and, finger to lips, cautioned Mary and Edward to silence. In the ensuing hush the sound of approaching footsteps could be plainly heard. "The King," said Catherine and adjusted her hood. Mary did the same and both women stood looking at the door for a moment with something like apprehension on their faces. Catherine, as though afraid of being caught idle, beckoned to Edward to resume his writing and standing behind his stool, leaned over to watch his progress.

Henry broke in upon this cosy domestic scene and surveyed his little family affably. Catherine and Mary curtsied and Edward rose again to bow, resuming his seat immediately. Henry inquired after affairs at Hunsdon and Mary talked to him of the doings of the household there. Her black mare had foaled she told him, and she had bought two spaniel dogs. Mary Browne was seeking permission to marry. Henry nodded agreeably as she detailed each little unimportant event and then said cheerfully, "And you, daughter? What have you been doing?"

Mary laughed. "Naught at which you would marvel, Father," she answered. "Reading, writing, practising the latest airs on my regals, strumming on my lute."

Catherine looked up from her inspection of Edward's work and said almost coyly, "I am writing a book, Mary. 'Tis to be called *The Lamentations of a Sinner* and is intended as a guide to the seemly conduct of married women. I wonder that you, who are so erudite do not try your hand at a little creative writing."

Mary said without thinking, "I am no Thomas More." The reference was unfortunate. Henry's good-natured expression vanished to be replaced by an ominous knitting of the brows. Quickly Catherine bridged the awkward silence. "If you do not think yourself capable of creative writing," she said hastily, "why not try translating some goodly work. There are many such which would be of benefit to mankind if translated from the Latin or Greek into English. Erasmus's *Paraphrases of the Gospel of St. John* for instance."

Mary's eyebrows shot up a good half-inch. She knew that Catherine had a leaning towards the Protestant Reformers and liked her none the less for it, but surely she could see that the translation of such a work would be treading dangerously near the realms of heresy.

Catherine was pulling something from the sleeve of her gown, her famous 'windows', two square pieces of glass bound together with wire and attached to a stick. She applied this contraption to her eyes the better to see Edward's work. Mary saw a chance to change the subject and seizing the windows from Catherine, put them up to her own eyes and made comic twists with her mouth at Edward. He screeched with delight.

'You may laugh at my windows, Mary," said Catherine, half laughing herself, "but you could do worse than let Master Dunne, my chaplain, make some for you. Your sight is quite as poor as mine. Short sight is the penalty we studious women pay for our learning."

Mary returned the contraption to Catherine and jumped nervously as her father, who had been watching her closely, said shortly, "You will carry out the translation for the Queen, daughter."

Mary stared at him in amazement. "B . . . but Father," she protested, "m . . . my Latin . . . I do not think my Latin is good enough for me to be able to translate the paraphrases."

"Nonsense." The royal voice was sharp.

Oh God, thought Mary with swift perception, he wants me to do this so that he can put me in the wrong again. Accuse me of heresy, have a permanent stick with which to beat me. Miserably she stared at Henry, her eyes somewhere in the region between his gold neck chain and the belt of his green velvet doublet. "I will do the translation, Father," she said meekly. "When I return to Hunsdon I doubt not but I shall find time somehow to . . ."

"You will do it here at Greenwich," Henry interrupted her harshly. "You will prolong your visit for the purpose."

Edward dropped his quill and clapped his hands. "Oh good, good," he chirped. "Mary is to stay at court!"

Mary smiled weakly at him, glad that he had entirely missed the implications of the conversation. Henry was already moving towards the door. "While you are here, Mary," he threw back over his shoulder, "you may sit for Master Ambrosius Benson the painter. 'Tis long enough since your likeness was painted. I should like a full-length portrait of you and this time I have in mind too a large family portrait, myself and the Queen with Edward, Elizabeth and yourself beside me. Master Benson has already done the sketches of Elizabeth and Edward. There remains now only yourself. He has sketches enough of me God knows and the Queen has but recently been painted by him, but the one of you by Master Holbein which hangs in the long gallery is fifteen years old."

Yes, thought Mary grimly, because for fifteen years I have not been worth the cost of the canvas and the brushes. She said nothing, however, merely curtsied to her father as he went out and returned to continue her study of Edward's work.

2

So Mary stayed at court and did the translation with Henry literally breathing over her shoulder. He passed several ominous-sounding remarks which made the flesh on the back of her neck crawl. "See how I am surrounded by learned women," he said one day. "Such persons must be watched, lest they tend towards heresy," and again, "I have noticed how women with heretical leanings are often barren. It is as though God were displeased with them for their unseemly inquisitiveness." This last was said with a sly glance at Catherine, who was present on this particular occasion with her ladies, and busy about the embroidering of a new cope for Archbishop Cranmer. Catherine did not look up from her work but her cheeks reddened and Mary saw how the hand holding her needle quivered slightly. "My mistress, Anne Boleyn," Henry went on relentlessly, "was sympathetic to the Reformers. She was not very fertile. She bore me but one living bastard."

Ah, Father, how can you? thought Mary as she plodded on with her task. How can you rake over those dead embers? She was shocked that Henry did not find reference to Anne Boleyn embarrassing, but apparently he did not. She wondered if he was quite right in the head these days. She was worried about Catherine who did not seem to sense that her leaning towards Protestantism was placing her in some danger. That, coupled with her apparent infertility were making Henry think in terms of being rid of her. This much was becoming obvious, even to the least observant member of the court. The burning question was how would Henry go about it? Another divorce? Another charge of adultery? A charge of heresy perhaps? Mary decided that she must warn Catherine to be discreet over the matter of her religion. Of course, Henry had come to rely on her to dress his infected leg which had never healed after a jousting fall. It was a loathsome task which even his gentlemen were reluctant to perform for him, but Catherine did it uncomplainingly, seeming not to notice the frightful smell which emanated from the wound when old bandages were removed and fresh ones applied. All the same he might, if he thought her barren, take another wife.

Mary found refreshing relief from all these tensions in her sittings with the painter Ambrosius Benson, a garrulous fellow who kept her in fits of laughter as he regaled her with the unimportant though scandalous gossip of the court. He would stand before his sketching block, which he had set up on an easel for greater convenience, with a stick of charcoal poised and then, just as she thought he was about to commence work, his head would dart forth from behind the easel and he would come out with some outrageous remark such as, "My lady, did you know that the Countess of Arundel has three moles on her belly big as pennies?"

Mary had actually giggled. "How can you know that, Master Benson?"

"Why certes, did not the lady tell me so herself and say she wished I could portray them on my canvas for posterity? She told me that they are so arranged that they look like the Medici coat of arms."

Mary had thrown back her head to roar with laughter. Benson had regarded her appreciatively. "You look so beautiful when you laugh, my lady. You should do it more often. Your face has too much solemnity. It is good to laugh is it not?"

"Yes, Master Benson, 'tis good to laugh," Mary had agreed fervently.

"I shall convey you so in the portrait."

"Oh, I do not think his grace the King would like that."

"No, perhaps not," Benson had conceded gloomily. "However, we will try a little curve of the lips to suggest a smile and we shall show quite a lot of that exquisite red hair of yours."

"Well perhaps that would be permitted."

"I painted your mother once when I was very young," Benson had confided. "A very great lady. She did me much honour when she gave me such an important commission." He smiled gently as he remembered. "She knew I was short of money you see. No one wanted my poor services when they could employ those of the great Master Hans Holbein." He shrugged and gave a little sigh. "Alas, the Queen did not like the portrait when it was done. She said I flattered her, but believe me, my lady, it was not so. Your lady mother was too modest. She made me destroy my work which, of course, saddened me. She paid me though. Oh yes indeed. I received my full fee."

Mary had sobered, her light mood dispelled by this poignant reminder of her mother. It was so like Catherine to abhor even a hint of flattery. She had cheered up when

Benson went on to talk of the Countess of Shrewsbury's right ear which he said started to waggle when she had drunk too much wine. She was soon laughing hysterically, holding her sides with the effort to control herself. She had been sorry when her sittings were over. There was no one like Master Benson for making one feel pleased with oneself. Of course, he had had much practice with all the court ladies and gentlemen he had painted.

3

Five weeks after she had come to court Mary finished her translation and presented it to Catherine who thanked her rather embarrassedly for she had had no idea what trouble her innocent suggestion would cause for Mary. She knew that Mary did not blame her for Henry's perversity, but this did not lessen her feeling of being responsible for the girl's discomfiture. Henry was all benevolence now that the task was done. He congratulated Mary on her command of Latin, indeed it had been a difficult translation, and promised her that before she left court she should see the unveiling of Master Benson's picture, now almost completed, which was to take place in the great hall.

On the day of the unveiling all the court assembled. The canvas was set up on the dais, covered with a linen cloth, and the master himself, when all were suitably attentive, removed the covering with a flourish. Quite two minutes passed before anyone noticed anything, but then, mingled with the usual admiring remarks, Mary heard one of the ladies nearest to her mutter, "God's love, the Queen!" She peered at the canvas, walking a little nearer so that she might get a better view. There was Henry, the central figure, seated on his chair of state, with Catherine beside him and herself, Edward and Elizabeth a little to one side on the right. The woman had mentioned the Queen. Mary looked at the figure of Catherine again and then she saw it. The gown was undoubtedly Catherine's and the jewellery. She was wearing the identical ensemble at the moment, but the face was not. The face belonged to Jane Seymour. Mary glanced at Benson. He caught her eye and shrugged miserably. He had had his orders the gesture seemed to say. All around Mary people were muttering low-voiced comments. It was not difficult to guess what they were saying. That the King was displeased with his barren wife and had therefore decided that she should not appear in the portrait. Instead he had had substituted the features of Jane Seymour, the only woman who had borne him a son.

Mary saw her father beckoning to her and went across to him where he stood under a painted window bearing the Beaufort arms. A white-faced Catherine almost cowered beside him. Henry looked at Mary intently. "How like you the portrait, Mary?"

"Very well indeed, Father," replied Mary brightly. "Master Benson has caught all our likenesses marvellous well."

"How like you his portrait of the Queen?"

"A speaking likeness," replied Mary loudly and stared her father straight in the eye. The small, darting orbs dropped before her own and she realised with surprise that she had put him to shame. He grunted and then, as though looking for some way to pay her back said, "I have ill news for you, daughter. Your friend Messire Eustace Chapuys is being recalled. He is not up to his job any more. Suffers from gout I believe."

Mary's fierce disappointment did not show on her face. She was used to masking her feelings now. "May I take my leave of him?"

"You will have to be quick about it," replied Henry, a gleam of unworthy triumph in his eyes. "He's away for Spain tomorrow."

It was on the tip of Mary's tongue to say, "You might have told me sooner, Father," but she thought that she had probably offended him sufficiently for one day and she held her peace.

She managed to convey to Chapuys at supper that she would meet him in the walled garden that night at nine of the clock. He nodded delightedly, for he had thought he was doomed to leave court without bidding her *adieu.* As the bells of the courtyard clock chimed, Mary descended the outside stair and made her way to the garden. The night air was cold and she drew her cloak tightly about her. She carried no flambeau in her hand, but she could see her way well enough by the light of the moon. Chapuys was waiting for her. He came towards her, hands outstretched to clasp hers. "My princess," he murmured. "It makes me sad to leave you."

"I too am sad, and sorry to see you go, Messire," Mary replied gently. She had a genuine affection for Chapuys which might, in other circumstances, have blossomed into love, but she was much older now than the frightened girl who had crouched beside the altar with the Savoyard in the chapel of Eltham manor, and knew that they could not have allowed their love to grow. He knew it too and was desolate because he did not think there would be any other woman in his life. For years he had protected her, looked to her interests, comforted her when she was in fear. Theirs had been a very special relationship, one which he would remember to his dying day.

She put into his hand a miniature of herself painted by Holbein when she was ten years old. It had been a very good likeness. She recalled with amusement how disgruntled the fat little German had been at having to make the long journey from London to Ludlow for the purpose. The miniature was set in a gold frame studded with diamonds and hung from a gold chain linked together with lustrous black pearls. Chapuys pressed it to his mouth and for a fleeting moment Mary wished that she could have substituted her own lips for the painted ones of the miniature. She took the trinket from him and carefully hung it about his neck. The tears in his eyes shone bright as crystal in the moonlight.

"My dear, dear Eustace," she murmured, "what am I to do without you?" and indeed she did feel disconsolate as she thought that his comforting, rock-like presence was about to be removed from her for ever.

The emotion-charged moment might even then have led them to indiscretion had not Mary's sharp ears picked up a faint rustling sound amongst the evergreen leaves of a near-by cherry laurel bush. Wriothesley, she thought, angrily. That foul little spy Wriothesley, time-serving wretch that he is. Mary hated Thomas Wriothesley, who had been promoted by Henry to the high office of Lord Chancellor after the death of Thomas, Lord Audley. He had more or less taken Thomas Cromwell's place and had proved a good watchdog for his master. Well, she would give him naught much to tattle about tonight. Henry could hardly upbraid her for presenting Chapuys with a gift. It was the customary thing to do anyway. Chapuys, conscious that her attention had been diverted from him, looked at her shrewdly.

"Wriothesley!" hissed Mary and took his arm. Defiantly, side by side, they marched out of the walled garden.

RICHMOND–HUNSDON

Autumn, 1548–June, 1549

I

The King was dead and had gone to his rest beneath the choir of St. George's Chapel, Windsor. There had been no more wives for him. His widow had cast off her purple mourning gown with disgraceful celerity to marry her first love, Thomas Seymour, Jane Seymour's younger brother. Mary had been shocked at the time, but now Catherine was dead, having borne a girl child whom she had named after her stepdaughter, and it was all water under the bridge.

It was the autumn of 1548 and Mary was with the court at Richmond. She had come for the purpose of seeing Edward, who had been ill with chicken-pox, and had asked for her presence to comfort him. She could not hesitate when that pale wraith of a boy needed her and so she had made the uncomfortable journey from Newhall manor in Essex, her new home since Henry's death, enduring the slanting autumn rain and the sharp wind which teased her ear-lobes and reddened her nose.

Edward was still very weak when she arrived and she was only able to spend short periods of time in his company lest she tire him, but he begged her to stay at court until he was quite recovered and she could not bear to refuse him though she felt uneasy. The atmosphere at court was distinctly and unequivocally 'Protestant'. Most of the members of Edward's newly-appointed Council were of the New Faith, all the old Catholic nobles having been banished. The ancient rites of the Catholic church were being banned. Processions, dirges and candles were going out of fashion and in parish churches all over the country the colourful wall paintings which told stories of the saints and tales from the Old and New Testaments, were being daubed and obliterated with whitewash. Soon Parliament were going to pass an Act of Uniformity which would make the use of Cranmer's new English Prayer Book compulsory. The celebration of Mass was to be abolished and at the service of communion it was to be understood that the bread and wine were merely symbols instead of the living Body and Blood of Christ. All these things worried Mary because she feared that Edward's Council would try to make her conform and conform she would not. It looked to her as though she was in for another long, weary struggle.

In the intervals when she was not with Edward, Mary hunted and rode with her ladies, but after she had been at court a week the weather turned so foul that she was forced to resort to walking in the long gallery and playing interminable games of cards. She always played for high stakes and invariably lost. Soon she was having to delve deep into her privy purse to pay her debts. Card-playing beginning to pall at last, she went in search of reading matter. She knew there would be books a-plenty in Edward's schoolroom and so one afternoon, when she had made twenty-four turns down the long gallery, she decided to see if Edward had a copy of the tragedies of Seneca. If his studies were following along the same lines as her own he almost certainly would she decided. Cheerfully declining the assistance of her ladies Mary left the long gallery. She did not notice a tall, blond-haired figure follow her out and almost cried aloud when she turned to find Thomas Seymour at her elbow. He placed a somewhat proprietary and intimate hand on her arm and guiding her towards the schoolroom said gaily, "Books, my lady. I'll lay wager you are after books to relieve your boredom."

"H . . . how did you guess, my lord?" asked Mary faintly.

Seymour flashed her his charming smile. "I have made it my business to discover what pleases your highness."

"Oh." Mary drew away from him slightly, disconcerted by his use of the forbidden title and Seymour, quick to sense the withdrawal, and the reason for it, was all deference. Gravely he bowed her into the schoolroom and hastened to find a stool for her. "If you will but tell me which books you want," he said, "I shall find them for you."

Despite herself Mary responded to Seymour's friendly manner. It was perhaps not so hard to understand why Queen Catherine had fallen so deeply in love with such a man and had defied all convention by marrying him but a few weeks after Henry's death. Her father must have been difficult at the last and Catherine glad to be free. She sat down on the stool and looked up at Seymour with a half-smile on her face. "I think one will suffice for the moment," she said. "I would like the tragedies of Seneca if there be a copy." She added, "Try that shelf. I believe Edward keeps his works of the classical poets there." Her hand indicated the topmost of a row of shelves which lined one wall. Seymour found the volume quickly and placed it in her hands. Mary fingered the worn vellum and opening the cover saw in Edward's thin handwriting, "This Book belongs to Edward the Kynge." She felt the prick of tears behind her eyelids and kept her head lowered. Instantly Seymour was on his knees before her. "You are sad, your grace?"

She raised her head and looked into bluer than blue eyes and a long distant chord sounded in her memory. The Emperor had such eyes and he had been kind to her. All at once Mary had an overwhelming desire to confide her troubles to this man who regarded her with such obvious sympathy. The impudent eyes in the lean, handsome face were faintly inquiring, the wide, sensual mouth half-open, expectant. Mary plunged. "I am worried sore about Edward's health," she said. "He is so weak and pale and does not seem to be making any progress at all after the pox. They make him study too hard, of course. Do you know, my lord, when he went to his crowning he could scarce support the crown on his head and when they gave him a purse full of gold pieces he complained of its weight."

"Aye, aye, so he did poor wight. As I remember it the purse was presented to him by the Lord Mayor before he entered the Abbey and he begged the Lord Chancellor to take it from him."

Seeing her dismal expression he said, "Your grace, from henceforth you may rest easy. I am as you know, often about the court. My duties as Lord High Admiral make it necessary for me to be so." Here Seymour's chest seemed to swell a little. "I shall look to the King's welfare on your behalf. I should consider it an honour."

"Oh, would you, my lord? Would you indeed? You have my everlasting gratitude."

Swiftly he was on his feet and rummaging in a high corner cupboard fixed to the wall, where Edward's tutor, Master John Cheke, kept his store of wine. "Let us drink to my promise, your grace," he said laughing at her over his shoulder. "Promises mean naught lest they be pledged in good wine and to be frank with you I find the Protestant air which hangs over this court a little too sobering. The dullards have even ordered that the wine shall be watered so that none of us shall be in danger of slipping under the supper board."

"And I have not been permitted to play my regals," said Mary quickly.

Fiercely Seymour banged down two pewter drinking pots on to the table and filled them to the brim from a half-gallon flagon containing pale green Marsala. He pushed one towards Mary and frowned. "I will not have it," he said, "that music is ungodly, and the food of the devil."

Mary was mildly amused. She drank from the goblet, eyeing Seymour over the rim. "Is that what the Reformers say?"

"That among other things," replied Seymour gloomily.

"You do not agree with their views?"

A flicker of caution showed in the blue eyes as Seymour lounged negligently against the table drinking his wine. "Well, I do not agree with everything. One has to compromise. My brother Edward, having been appointed Protector during the King's minority, I have to tread warily. Compromise. You know how it is."

"Yes, I know how it is," said Mary quietly, remembering a far-off day at Hunsdon when she had compromised for the last time. She thought about the tall, quiet man with the mouse-brown beard who had come with the others to Hunsdon on the day of her ignoble submission to her father's will. An ambitious man indeed, though he had not looked so. He was now Edward, Duke of Somerset, Protector of the Realm.

"I am a good Catholic at heart," Seymour was saying, for he had noticed a slight disdainfulness in her manner following his last pronouncement, "and I warrant half the members of the Council are too, though they profess to adhere to the New Faith."

"All the old Catholic peers are gone," said Mary, draining her goblet, "and Norfolk is in the Tower along with Bishops Gardiner and Bonner, God keep them."

She was becoming too morose. To lighten her mood Seymour refilled her goblet and reverted to the subject of her music. "It distresses me to think that they have denied you the pleasure of your music," he said. "If you feel you grow out of practice I can send you my man Walter Earle to give you some lessons. He is greatly skilled on the lute, virginals and regals. Just say the word and he shall be yours for as long as you want him."

The heady wine was beginning to have its effect on Mary.

She experienced a pleasant lassitude in her limbs and she felt carelessly inconsequent. "Thank you, my lord," she replied, smiling up at him. "I may well accept your kind offer."

He brought a stool so that he might sit beside her. His eyes embraced her with flattering, soothing warmth. She felt a quick flutter of excitement and her heart began to beat faster. A slow flush crept up from her neck to inflame her cheeks. He moved his stool a little nearer, watching her with the same careful intensity of a cat at a mousehole. Wildly she searched her brain for something to discuss which would break the taut moment. She found only her religion. "They will forbid my Mass," she said abruptly. "When Parliament passes the new law. 'Tis to be called the Act of Uniformity, I think?" Her voice cracked as it rose on the query and Seymour nodded briefly, still fixing her with his smothering stare. "I . . . I . . . do not know what . . . er, what will happen," Mary stumbled on. "Edward. Well he is a mere boy, and steeped since birth in the ways of the Reformers. Why, he has even s . . . s . . . seen f . . . f . . . fit to remonstrate with me about my Mass." The old stammer was back again and she cursed her tripping tongue.

Seymour made soothing noises and filled her goblet for the third time. "I will see that you keep your Mass, your grace," he promised her confidently. "I will speak to my brother on the matter."

Mary's eyes swam with tears of gratitude. "Oh, will you, my lord? I fear me I should die were they to take away my Mass. 'Tis the only thing that makes life bearable for me."

"Poor lass," murmured Seymour and stroked her face gently. He leaned even closer and she inhaled the sandalwood perfume he used on his beard. Delicious, dizzying waves of it wafted towards her and made her head swim. She swayed towards him and he put his hands on her shoulders. "You need a husband, highness," he whispered. "A proper man to protect you and keep you warm of nights."

Mary's colour deepened.

"Even his grace the King realises your need," persisted Seymour. "Why, only the other day he asked me whether I should marry again and when I said I thought not—well, what think you the King said?"

Mary shook her head dumbly, but a small note of warning sounded in her brain. Seymour's hands were moving down her arms and one was creeping round to support her back. "The King said, your grace, that *you* were in need of a husband."

"Did he so?" replied Mary thickly, ignoring the warning and blatantly offering him her mouth. The next instant they would have been locked in each other's arms had not the door opened and a small figure appear, to stand framed beneath the arch. Innocently, the young girl advanced into the chamber, seeing naught amiss in the attitude of the two figures seated near the table. The Lady Jane Grey, great-niece of the late King Henry, daughter of Henry Grey, Marquis of Dorset and ward of Thomas Seymour, Baron Seymour of Sudeley, addressed her guardian in a clear ringing voice, failing to see that he was showing unmistakable signs of bad temper.

"My lord," she said, "I have been searching the palace for you to return this." She held out a bundle of parchments, roughly bound together to form a book. The light from the painted window played on the slender figure in its plain gown of dark blue velvet. She wore no jewellery and the beautiful ash-blonde hair was almost entirely concealed beneath her ornamented hood. Almost exactly the same age as her cousin King Edward, having been born in the same month of the same year, the Lady Jane looked older. Years of study, carried out under tremendous pressure from brutal parents, had made of her a woman before her time.

Seymour almost snatched the book from the child and would have turned his back on her but she touched him timidly on the shoulder and smiling her sweet smile which transformed the plain young face into something purely beautiful she said, "I have read every word, my lord, and I swear your views are more advanced than those of good Master Udall." Nicholas Udall was a noted Reformer.

Despite her befuddled state Mary became instantly alert. She rose unsteadily to her feet, shaking off Seymour's supporting hand. Clutching the edge of the table she glared at him glassily. "If you are seeking a new wife, my lord," she snapped, "try the Lady Elizabeth. She is more to your taste I'll warrant with her Protestant ways," and then, as he remained silent, for once at a loss and finding nothing to say to counter her anger, "but, of course, that maidenhead may have come your way already." This was a reference to the time when Elizabeth had lived in Seymour's household, during his brief marriage to Catherine Parr, when all the world knew they had conducted the most unseemly romps together.

Seymour's eyes popped with fury, but he was no match for an angry Tudor and stood helpless and fuming as Mary took her indignant leave.

2

Thomas Seymour was dead. His searing ambition, which had led him to think he might marry a Tudor, had killed him. The Bishop of Lincoln's chaplain, on his way north, stopped at Hunsdon for refreshment and a bed for the night and told Mary that he had died terribly, resisting the executioner. Pity dispelled anger and in the privacy of her chamber Mary wept for him. At Hatfield the Lady Elizabeth, who had been roused to physical awareness by the handsome Seymour, bit her pallid lip and commented, "This day died a man of much wit and very little judgement." This was in the spring of 1549. Soon afterwards Mary heard that the Act of Uniformity was law and was to be enforced that Whitsuntide. From Hunsdon she wrote to Protector Somerset, taking issue with him about altering the state of religion in England contrary to the terms of her father's will. Somerset, prompted by John Dudley, Earl of Warwick, who was soon to step into his shoes, replied to the effect that her words "sounded not well to his ears" and that commissioners in the persons of Lord Chancellor Rich, Thomas Wriothesley, now Earl of Southampton, and the Earl of Warwick would be coming to her at Whitsuntide to see that she obeyed the Act.

John Dudley, thought Mary, scanning the letter. I have not seen him for years. It is hard to believe that he was once my Chamberlain, all those years ago at Ludlow Castle. How he has risen in the world! She had an interview with Spain's new ambassador, Messire Van der Delft, who told her that the Emperor Charles was doing all within his power to see that she was allowed to keep her Mass. With that she had to rest content, but as Whitsuntide approached, fear, as so often before, became her bed-mate. The night before the arrival of the commissioners she slept not at all and met them the next morning with drawn face and aching head. Lord Chancellor Rich, young for his high office, pale and pimply, with a round moon face like soft candle wax, opened the stormy, hour-long meeting with the words, "You know what we have come about, lady."

"Do I?" inquired Mary irritatingly.

Rich grunted and smoothed his oily black beard. He had been told that the Lady Mary would be difficult so he supposed that all the due forms would have to be observed. From the sleeve of his over-gown he took a copy of the Act of Uniformity and solemnly intoned all the articles in his high nasal voice. Mary listened in silence and when Rich had finished asked calmly, "And what has this to do with me?"

Enraged by her air of slightly amused tolerance, which masked, had he but known it, an inner apprehension such as she had never experienced before, Rich lost his temper. "You are to observe it lady, observe it!" he snarled. "That is what it has to do with you!"

"I will not give up my Mass," said Mary stubbornly.

John Dudley, Earl of Warwick, stepped forward and smiled placatingly at her. Mary stared gravely back at him. He had not changed much, save that his hair and beard were speckled with grey and his short figure had run to fat. Apart from that he was still the same saucy fellow who had teased her aunt all that time ago. "My lady," he was saying, his voice wheedling, "we on the Council are all good Catholics like yourself, but we have come to realise that some of the old forms are no longer to be desired. I like not the term 'Protestant'. It smacks of rebellion. Rather would I use the word 'progressive'. We prefer to worship God with simpler ceremonial, doing away with images, candles and the like. There is naught so much amiss with that is there?"

Mary's eyes blazed. How dare this upstart earl dispose thus of God's true religion in a few facile words. "You make it sound so innocent, my lord," she flared, "this new religion of yours, but can you tell me that you have not denied the living presence of Christ at the communion table. Can you tell me that there are not those among you who deride the holy wafer, saying it is not Christ's Blessed Body and sneer that the baker made it? Can you tell me that you get comfort from a communion where you think of Christ's Body as humble bread?"

"Ah, transubstantiation, we are back to that," said Dudley nodding sagely.

"Certes, we are back to that!" shouted Mary, beside herself with rage now. " 'Tis the hub and essence of the matter and the main reason why I abhor this vile religion of yours and why I will never, never, while I have breath in my body, subscribe to it."

They wrangled on for another thirty minutes until Mary, her head bursting, brought the meeting to a close by saying, "You have my answer, my lords. You may take it back to London with you and discuss it in Council. Then perhaps you will let me know whether or not I am to be arrested for heresy."

Rich wiped his streaming brow, Dudley looked at his boots and Wriothesley, who had taken very little part in the argument, fell to coughing. He was suffering from inflammation of the lungs which was to kill him within the year. They took their leave of her and when they were gone she sent word to Van der Delft to come to her at Hunsdon. She had taken a momentous decision. She would ask the Spanish ambassador to help her flee the country, for she was certain now that her persecutors would pursue her to the grave.

WOODHAM WALTER–COPT HALL

July, 1550–August, 1551

I

The Privy Council, thinking to break Mary's spirit, disbanded her household at Hunsdon and moved her to the small, draughty manor house of Woodham Walter, near Maldon in Essex. They were unaware that they were putting the means of escape closer to hand. Mary had spoken to Van der Delft, who in turn had spoken to the Emperor, and it had been arranged that she should go across to Flanders.

The escape plan was fairly simple. Woodham Walter being close to the river Blackwater, Mary was to wait in the manor house for the Emperor's envoy, one Jean Dubois, who would take her and two of her ladies in a small boat down river to the estuary where would be waiting a larger Spanish vessel to which they would transfer for the journey across the Channel. The Emperor had decreed that the escape should be attempted after dark in the middle of the month of June. Van der Delft would inform Mary of the exact date. He had done so and now she was waiting in her chamber at Woodham Walter, pacing the floor and absently telling her beads while Susan Clarencieux and Jane Dormer, the two ladies she had selected to come with her, were tying into bundles the barest necessities for the journey.

Mary stopped her pacing and addressing Susan said, "What if Messire Dubois' boat is stopped by the watch or the bailiff at Maldon?"

Susan, whose round, rosy face had thinned in the harassing service of her mistress and whose brown hair was now tinged with grey, answered reassuringly, "Messire Dubois is to have corn in the hold of his boat. If the watch stop him he will say that he has come to sell it in Maldon town. They will believe him, Madam, have no fear. Plenty of corn boats ply up and down the Blackwater."

Mary's brow creased into a frown. She would not have admitted it for the world, but she was beginning to regret her decision to flee from England. It had seemed the only course open to her at the time, but now she was not so sure. Perhaps she could have held the Council at bay for a while to give herself time to think. "What if the bailiff is suspicious?" she asked aloud. "What if he questions Dubois too closely?"

Jane Dormer finished tying one bundle and straightening, rubbed her aching back. She smiled broadly at Mary, and purposely evading her question, said, "Just think, Madam, by this time tomorrow we shall all be under the protection of his grace the Emperor. Then will we have naught more to fear."

Mary did not reply. She bit her lip worriedly. "Dubois is late," she said. "Perhaps he is already taken."

At that moment there came a sharp rap on the door which made her jump with fright. Her Comptroller, Sir Robert Rochester, entered. He looked vaguely anxious, but to Mary's over-excited imagination he seemed as though about to impart the most doleful tidings. She clapped both hands to her head and moaned, "Oh Jesu, Master Comptroller, what's amiss? Your face tells me you have bad news."

"No, no, Madam." Rochester tried to calm her. "But something has just passed which may put a different complexion on things."

"How so?"

Rochester mopped his brow, for the night was warm. He was a small, skinny man with rabbit teeth and black eyes which almost met at the bridge of his nose. He saw Mary looking at him impatiently and hastened to enlighten her. "There is a squire below," he said, "craving shelter for the night. He is in the service of the Earl of Warwick and is on his way to Colchester with a message. It seems he has come directly from the court where the King is recovering from a rheum. The physician who attended his grace told this young man, most indiscreetly I thought, that the King will not live above four years longer. He says he will never live to marry and beget children."

The information did not take Mary completely by surprise. More and more lately had she noticed the change in Edward, the way the boy was constantly ill and how he spent more time in bed than out of it. "I know he is not strong," she said quietly.

Rochester waved his hands at her. "Madam, do you not see what this means? In the very near future you are likely to be Queen. Under the terms of your gracious father's will you follow King Edward in the line of succession. The Privy Council have been able to do naught to alter that, disregard though they have many of the other clauses."

"You . . . you mean I should stay?" Mary's voice was half-fearful, half-hopeful and Rochester, who had known for long that her heart was only half-set on the matter of escape, put forward the one argument which he knew would stay her. "If you leave the country, Madam, England will never be restored to the Church of Rome."

Rochester, a fervent Catholic, really believed what he said. He had been very much against the venture from the first. Mary burst into floods of tears. They were tears of relief. She was still wiping her eyes with her kerchief when Dubois was announced. Immediately, she fell into a panic. "Oh what shall I do?" she wailed. "I cannot see the Emperor's envoy like this. Tell him to wait, Master Comptroller, until I am more composed. Conduct him to . . ." But it was too late. Dubois was already in the chamber and gazing at her curiously. He bowed hurriedly to her. Though he had never seen her before he could not doubt that this small, distressed, red-haired woman was a Tudor. "Your Majesty," he said, "you must come at once, before the tide turns."

Mary fluttered at the unfamiliar title. She had forgotten that to Imperialists she was Queen of England now that her father was dead, because they recognized only his marriage to Catherine, which had taken place before his break with the Church of Rome. "I . . . er . . . I am not ready," she said. "Will not tomorrow serve as well?" She looked desperately at Rochester for help for she could not bring herself to tell Dubois who, after all, had obviously gone to a deal of trouble on her behalf, that his dangerous mission had been in vain. To her consternation Rochester chose that precise moment to hurry out of the chamber.

"Wh . . . what about all my effects?" Mary asked Dubois wildly. "I cannot go a pauper to my cousin the Emperor. I must have time, Messire Dubois . . . time . . ." Her voice trailed off as she fingered her beads.

Jean Dubois scratched his smooth, dark head and said puzzledly, "But, Madam, the Emperor will give you everything you need. He has ordered me to see that you want for nothing when we get to Flanders."

Mary shook her head emphatically. "No, no, I would be

too ashamed to take anything from him. He has done so much already."

Dubois was obviously at a loss. He muttered disappointedly, "As Your Majesty pleases."

Mary felt sorry for him and was just about to offer him some wine when Rochester returned with some 'information'. It was to the effect that the watch had been doubled that night and that it was far too dangerous for Mary to attempt the escape.

Dubois shrugged resignedly. "What do you want me to do?" he asked.

Rochester started to hustle him out of the chamber. "I have arranged for an escort to take you back to your boat, Messire Dubois," he said. "I fear you must return to Flanders until a more opportune time can be arranged for her grace to leave England."

Which will be never, thought Dubois with some annoyance. He remembered his manners in time to bow to Mary and ask her if she had any messages she wished him to convey to the Emperor.

"J . . . just my thanks, Messire Dubois," said Mary lamely, "m . . . my . . . grateful thanks." And my thanks to you too, Rochester, she thought. Her Comptroller's quick-wittedness had extricated her from an extremely embarrassing situation.

2

". . . and I will have my laws obeyed." Mary gave a snort of disgust and threw Edward's letter on to the floor. She recognised Dudley's hand in it. It was over a year now since she had almost made the escape attempt. Unhappily for her the Council had somehow found out about the proposed scheme and had begun a systematic persecution of all her household servants who heard Mass with her. Her almoner, one Francis Mallet, had fled to the north country and others had been removed from her household. Now Mary had no friends at court. Even Somerset, who had inclined to leniency towards her, was immured in the Tower awaiting arraignment on a charge of high treason at Westminster Hall. John Dudley, now promoted to the dukedom of Northumberland, had slipped swiftly into his shoes and things had got so bad that Mary in desperation had gone to court at Christmas of the year 1550 and had pleaded with Edward personally.

Her brother had opened the interview after a quick glance at Northumberland for guidance by saying that he had heard she habitually disobeyed the Act of Uniformity by hearing Mass. Mary, looking at the small worried figure seated on the over-large chair of state, had burst into tears. This had set Edward off and he had sobbed brokenly that he would never do anything to harm her. Now Edward had done an about-face, undoubtedly prompted by Northumberland, and in a four-page letter discussing her conduct, had informed her that he was sending commissioners to forbid all her household chaplains to say Mass and there let there be an end to the matter.

Mary groaned inwardly. Oh these ceaseless deputations. These men who rode to her manor houses and pestered the life out of her with their continual demands for her submission to some edict or other. Who was it this time? Irritably Mary retrieved the letter she had thrown down and sought for the names. Rich and Petre. Jesu, she hoped she could keep her temper with that paunchy fellow Rich. What a man to make Lord Chancellor with such a one as Stephen Gardiner, Bishop of Winchester, one of the keenest brains in England, rotting in the Tower. If ever she came to the throne . . . but she must not think of that. It would necessitate poor little Edward being dead. An unworthy thought.

Mary beckoned to Susan Clarencieux who was re-stringing her lute, a surprising skill she had learned from a travelling minstrel. Susan was swiftly at her side and curtsying. Mary smiled at her. "Go summon all the chaplains, Susan," she commanded, "and send them to me in the inner hall. I have something I wish to say to them."

Susan curtsied again, a worried expression on her face, and when she was gone Mary studied the letter once more in a vain attempt to find a loophole. There was none. Mass was to be forbidden altogether in her household by order of the Privy Council. She looked down at her everyday gown of cheap Bristol red with its under-gown of blue diaper. Some of the braiding was coming loose. She must tell Jane or Susan to sew it back again. No chance of purchasing a new one alas. Since her father's death she had been in poor case. He had left her no money. His bequests to her consisted of a few ill-kept manors in the eastern counties, Newhall, Kenninghall, Copt Hall, where she was now in residence, and Woodham Walter, a place for which she had understandably developed a slight distaste. Her father's initial generosity, when she had first submitted to his wishes and signed the Oath of Succession, had soon faded and she was for ever having to apply to the King's Comptroller for money which that tight-fisted gentleman handed out in niggling amounts of twenty crowns at a time. When it came to New Year's gifts Mary was forced to make quite a few herself which taxed both her eyesight and her temper. She had given away most of her jewellery in gifts and had at one time been put to the expedient of pawning some silver goblets to obtain money to give to one of her serving-women as a small marriage dowry. No money. No Mass. The latter would cause her infinitely more grief.

Mary made her way to the inner hall. The chaplains were arriving in ones and twos until at last all nine were assembled. Mary greeted them warmly as they stood before her in a bowing line. Briefly she gave them details of the King's command and their faces lengthened. Master John Hamley, only eighteen and but lately admitted to Holy orders, was the most vehement in his shocked protests. "I shall say Mass for you, Madam, whether they forbid me or not," he declared defiantly. "They may take my life for it."

Mary smiled at the tall, ungainly figure before her, clad in the over-large black gown, a hand-me-down from Father Mallet. "That you will not, John," she said. "I'll have none of my household suffer on my behalf."

"But, Madam," argued the eager youth, his lint-white hair standing up like straw, "I would hide my head in shame rather than that you should be denied your Mass." The other chaplains nodded solemnly and murmured agreement, taking courage from this valiant, importunate youth.

Mary had stiffened at his words and her grey eyes were gleaming. "Hide," she said thoughtfully. "Master John, you have just given me an idea which may save us all a deal of sadness. It seems to me that if one of you were to hide while the commissioners are here you could not hear the order not to say Mass and if you could not hear the order . . ." She left the sentence unfinished but they immediately followed her train of thought. "Let it be me! Me! Me!" they clamoured, vying with each other for this unexpected honour. Mary raised her hands for silence, shaking her head the while. "No, no, good sirs, you must draw lots, 'tis the only fair way and let me warn you, he who is thus chosen runs a great risk, for if he is discovered he may find himself in the Tower."

They disregarded her warning as totally unimportant.

One of them rushed out for some quills which were broken into various lengths and placed between the covers of a book with the ends protruding. He who chose the shortest length was to be the one to hide. The chaplains became quite animated about this little "game" and one would have thought that it was some Yuletide frolic. To his great joy Master Hamley chose the shortest piece. Mary looked at him ruefully. "I'll grant 'tis fitting, John, that the lot should fall to you, who gave me the idea, but I misdoubt me if we can find anywhere to accommodate that lanky frame of yours without some portion of it sticking out!"

In the end it was decided that the youth should lie behind the altar in the chapel until the commissioners had gone. Mary was fairly sure that neither Rich nor Petre would know the exact number of her chaplains, but she was equally certain that they would poke their noses into every hole and corner at Copt Hall, and it was therefore necessary to keep Master Hamley well out of sight.

The day appointed for the visitation arrived. To her annoyance Mary woke up with a bad headache. It made her irritable when she wanted to stay calm and composed for the commissioners. Her ladies dressed her in her carefully preserved best gown of green velvet trimmed with miniver, with an under-gown of gold brocade. Her hood was ornamented with gold filigree work and she wore on her finger the diamond ring given to her by Jane Seymour. She found that she was too agitated to break her fast after Mass, but she drank half a cup of wine to give herself courage and settled down with her needlework to wait for Rich and Petre. They came just before noon and she received them in the inner hall with all her ladies present. They gave her letters from the King which she accepted and read with deliberate slowness while they fidgeted and fumbled with their sword-belts.

Mary finished reading the letters at last and passing them to Jane Dormer to hold said coolly, "Well?"

Rich coughed and picked at a spot on his nose. "You understand the contents of the letters, my lady?"

"I can read, can I not?" snapped Mary.

Rich plodded on, ignoring her obvious ill humour. "You understand that you are no longer to hold Catholic services in this household and that only the new Protestant service can be permitted?"

"There will be no Protestant services at Copt Hall while I

lie under its roof," retorted Mary. "If 'tis your intent to force such a service upon me I shall leave the house and wander the countryside in a kirtle like any serving-wench."

"You will obey the King's commands," said Rich loudly.

"Aye, the King's commands," echoed Petre a trifle lamely.

Mary looked at the latter with contempt. Another fat Protestant. They fed themselves too well. Would not fast at the specified times like every good Christian should. Having thus dismissed Petre she turned again to Rich. "It is monstrous that you should force on me the whims of a fourteen-year-old boy," she said, "though I suspect that those same whims are prompted by others. Would you ask such a callow youth his opinion on matters of foreign policy? No, of a surety you would not."

Rich discounted these remarks and said stolidly, "The King is to appoint a new Comptroller for your household. Sir Robert Rochester is to be relieved of his duties, for he is a known trouble-maker and will incite your ladyship to disobey the laws of the King."

"If my Comptroller is to be removed I shall appoint a new one myself," replied Mary angrily. "I have always appointed my own servants and do not need your help in such a matter. And now, my lords, if you wish to issue certain orders to my chaplains, which I understand is the main purpose of your visit, I will bid you adieu. I am feeling far from well. When you have done your business you can get out. I shall offer you no hospitality." With this parting shot Mary took her leave.

Rich shouted after her, "You will regret this high-handed attitude, lady. The Privy Council are on good terms with France now. We do not need the help of your friend the Emperor Charles."

The arrow found its mark. Mary experienced a wave of nausea and to her shame she vomited before she could reach the silver basin in her chamber.

The chaplains were rounded up and solemnly charged by Rich not to say Mass. Though the Lord Chancellor, as Mary had anticipated, entered every part of the manor, including the chapel, he did not find Master Hamley who lay, rigid as a statue, behind the altar. Rich was not looking for anything in particular, but he had been requested by the Council to "observe keenly" and he did so. Satisfied at last that there was no smell of mischief about the place he and Petre prepared to depart.

Ashen-faced after her bout of sickness Mary ran to a window overlooking the courtyard to watch them go. As they mounted their horses she threw the casement wide and called out, "If you take my Comptroller, my lord Rich, you will get no yearly accounting from my household. The King and Queen, God assoil them, did not teach me to juggle with figures." And then, as Rich and Petre wheeled their horses, presenting her with broad, dumb backs, "God keep your souls, my lords. Your bodies are as fat as farrowing sows and past amending."

Mary's household servants, gathered below to watch the departure of the King's commissioners, looked up at the window where the red, irate head protruded far out into the courtyard and rocked with laughter. They had never before known their mistress to give way to such a barrage of undignified abuse. It did their hearts good. Mary was laughing herself as she disengaged the lappet of her hood from the casement latch and banged it shut.

PART THREE

"Crabbed age and youth cannot live together,
Youth is full of pleasaunce, age is full of care,
Youth like summer morn, age like winter weather,
Youth like summer brave, age like winter bare."
Shakespeare—*The Passionate Pilgrim.*

FRAMLINGHAM–LONDON

JULY, 1553

I

Mary reined in her black mare and peered ahead down the long, dust-caked road, above which hung a shimmering heat-haze. She beckoned to her Master of the Horse, Sir Anthony Browne, a sturdy gentleman of yeoman stock who had served her for ten years in one capacity or another. Nudging his horse alongside Mary's mare he bowed stiffly from the waist, awaiting her pleasure.

"How far to Hoddesdon, Sir Anthony?" asked Mary tiredly. At that moment Susan Clarencieux trotted up with a dampened face-clout for her mistress's use. Mary thanked her gratefully and scrubbed at her face. "God's love, but it's hot," she muttered.

Sir Anthony, with judiciously pursed lips, was shrewdly calculating how much farther they had to go. "I think, Madam, Hoddesdon be not more than six miles distant," he said.

"Thanks to the Blessed Virgin for that," replied Mary, handing the face-clout back to Susan. "We can stop there for the night, Sir Anthony. I shall drop with fatigue if I do not rest soon!"

"You have pushed yourself hard, Madam," said Sir Anthony, watching her keenly from under heavy black brows. "You think that the King is very sick?" he asked.

"I fear so," replied Mary worriedly. "Northumberland's letter bade me be yare, for Edward sore needed my presence."

Sir Anthony sighed. "I fear his grace is not strong."

"No, Sir Anthony, he is not strong," agreed Mary sadly. She touched the mare's ribs with her heels and the blown though worthy beast responded at once. The small company began to move forward again. Mary fumbled in the velvet bag tied to the pommel of her saddle and brought forth Northumberland's letter. She read it for the thousandth time. It was maddeningly vague. The duke had not disclosed the nature of Edward's ailment, merely that it was serious. The King needed her at his side, he wrote, and called for her constantly. Called for her? This sounded almost as though he were in some sort of delirious fit. Mary told herself that it was useless to fret at this juncture. She must get to court. Only then would she find out what ailed Edward. Another day's hard riding should do it, but stop at Hoddesdon she must, otherwise she would be ill herself.

The hot glare of the sun hurt her eyes and she kept her head lowered over the mare's neck. Five minutes later she looked up to blink some dust out of her eyes and saw a small grey cloud gathering and thickening on the road ahead. Sir Anthony was at her side again. "I think it be a single horseman," he said. Curiously they watched while the cloud of dust grew bigger and resolved itself into horse and rider who were covering the ground at break-neck speed. Suddenly the rider looked up and sighted their party. He reined in his horse until he had reduced the animal to a trot. Mary just had time to identify the rider as Sir Nicholas Throckmorton, her brother's Under-Treasurer, before he dismounted and leaving his horse to graze by the roadside, sped swiftly towards her and sinking to one knee grasped the mare's stirrup. Mary tugged at the mare's bridle. She could hardly believe her eyes. On her infrequent visits to court Throckmorton had barely given her courtesy and now here he was on one knee to her. Afterwards she was to wonder why she had been so slow-witted as not to have divined the significance of this.

Throckmorton, sweat pouring down his cheeks, struggling anguishedly for breath, managed at last to gasp out, "Madam, Your Majesty, the King is dead."

Mary crossed herself. "Oh Jesu . . . oh dear, sweet Jesu . . . I . . . how? . . ." Tears bade fair to choke her and she had to make a tremendous effort to retain her composure. "When?" she asked almost harshly.

"Two days ago in the forenoon, half an hour before Sext."

"Two days since?" said Mary incredulously, then tentatively, "Was it an easy passing? D . . . did he suffer?"

Throckmorton hesitated. The Queen looked in bad enough case already. How could he tell her that Edward had lain for days on the great bed in his chamber, a prey to agonising pain, the like of which he had never before witnessed and crying pathetically that he wanted his dearest Mary to come to him, for she would amend him. "His passing was easy, Madam," he lied and could not look her in the eye. She, who had had so much experience of false-tongued dissemblers, was quick to see that he lied, but she did not press him. She could not have borne to hear of Edward's sufferings now. Later, perhaps later, she would ask. Throckmorton was still bursting with news and she said wearily, "There is something more, Sir Nicholas?"

"Yes, Madam, much more," replied Throckmorton grimly. "You must proceed no farther towards London for the Duke of Northumberland has proclaimed your cousin, the Lady Jane Grey as Queen, or rather should I say the Lady Jane Dudley, for she is now wed to Northumberland's son Guilford."

Mary's face expressed shock. The members of her household gathered about her like a protective screen, their eyes fixed on Throckmorton's face. The disturbing nature of these tidings temporarily deprived Mary of the power of speech. Sir Edward Waldegrave, one of her gentlemen, spoke for her. "How can this be?" he asked, glaring at Throckmorton. "The late King Henry declared in his will that the princess's grace should succeed her brother to the throne."

"So he did," agreed Throckmorton, "but Northumberland got young King Edward to make a new will bequeathing the throne to the Lady Jane."

Mary found her voice. "But that is against the law," she declared. "Edward had no power to bequeath the crown."

Throckmorton was still kneeling. Absently she motioned him to rise. "When did my brother make his will?"

"On his deathbed, Madam."

The colour flamed in Mary's cheeks. "When he was sick and ill and most like in pain, Northumberland forced him to make a will?"

"Yes, Madam." Throckmorton did not add that he himself had pressed Edward's trembling fingers round the pen while he signed the infamous document, and had wiped away with his sleeve the tears of weakness which smudged the signature.

Mary said between clenched teeth. "If I come safely into my own, he shall pay for that with his life."

"And for his treachery to your grace," put in Sir Anthony Browne. There was a chorus of assent and when it subsided into vague murmurings Throckmorton said urgently, "Madam, you must return north at once and take refuge in one of your manors. Might I suggest Kenninghall. It is the largest and would, I think, be the most secure. When Northumberland sent for you to come to court the King was already dead. He thought to lure you into a trap and when you do not come he will send an army to take you."

"Has he that much support?" Mary was surprised and a little disappointed. She had thought the people would have shown more loyalty to the daughter of Henry Tudor.

"The duke has hauled up the Tower guns to the top of the White Tower in readiness for a possible attack," explained Throckmorton. "While he holds London his position is strong."

Mary looked at Throckmorton suspiciously. "How do I know that you speak truth? Methought you were Northumberland's man. I heard tell you two were mighty close."

Throckmorton looked uncomfortable. Mary's remark was very near the truth but he had been shrewd enough to see that the duke's coup was likely to fail because support for it on the Council was only lukewarm. "I like not traitors," he told Mary.

"Hmm, well, it seems to me that I must put my trust in you, Sir Nicholas, and if it is well-founded you shall be amply rewarded. I promise you that." She laughed harshly. "Your tale is almost too fantastic to be false."

Silently Throckmorton bowed, backed away and went to fetch his horse.

2

So the cavalcade turned northwards, going by the Newmarket and Thetford road. They stopped at Sawston Hall, home of one Master John Huddleston, a fervent Catholic, who gave them shelter for the night. In the morning Mary heard Mass for the first time as Queen of England, and there were none present who did not mark the solemnity with which she gazed on the Host and the lowly reverence she made before the altar. After Mass the party agreed to split up for greater safety and Mary went on alone to Kenninghall, mounted behind a servant of Master Huddleston's. Topping a rise three miles away the man reined in his horse and turning, looked back to see Sawston Hall going up in flames. It was apparent that the duke's men had already got wind of Mary's presence there and were hard on her heels. The servant wept as he spurred his horse forward and Mary squeezed his shoulder sympathetically. "When I come into my own I will build your master a new house," she promised.

The whole party arrived safely at Kenninghall. Mary was the last to come and smiled as cheerfully as she could at the worried faces assembled in the hall. She went at once to her presence chamber and calling for ink and pens wrote to the Council in London claiming her rights. As she sat there, scribbling furiously, Sir Anthony Browne came to tell her that already news was coming in of nobles riding to Kenninghall to support her cause. The Earl of Bath was but two miles distant with a company of soldiers. He had with him Sir Thomas Wharton and Sir Henry Bedingfield. At that very moment too, people from the surrounding villages were bringing in supplies of bread, fish, cheese and ale to fill the empty larders. He added on a note of caution that Northumberland's men were on the march and he was gathering quite a bit of support. It would be better therefore, if Mary moved on to Framlingham Castle as soon as she had despatched her letters to the Council. Mary groaned, but saw the wisdom of Sir Anthony's advice and the next day the household, together with the many new arrivals, moved on to Framlingham Castle, once the holding of the dukes of Norfolk until the family's fall from grace. The old Duke of Norfolk was still in the Tower under sentence of death, having been arrested in 1546 on a charge of high treason at the instigation of the Duke of Somerset, then Earl of Hertford. Only the passing of King Henry had saved him. Mary thought that the old warrior would not mind her making use of his castle until the issue was settled one way or the other, and if it turned in her favour she would hand Norfolk back his property with the greatest of pleasure and free him from the Tower to enjoy it.

Once at Framlingham Mary's spirits drooped. Activity had so far buoyed her up, but now there was naught left to do save wait. Not even any more letters she could usefully write. Sir Anthony Browne, seeing her depression, tried to cheer her. "All will be well, Madam. You may take my word on it. You are already being proclaimed all over the country."

"Yes, and as fast as my friends proclaim me in one town, Northumberland's supporters arrive, tear down the proclamation and proclaim my cousin Jane," replied Mary, a hint of amusement creeping into her voice. "At least, so I am informed by the last batch of messengers who arrived."

Suddenly they both saw the humour of this extraordinary situation and started to laugh. Mary's laughter was on the edge of hysteria, but she fought it down. "What happens if the two opposing parties come into the town square at the same time?" she giggled.

"They fight it out there and then I suppose," laughed Sir Anthony.

Yet another messenger, booted and spurred, came hurrying into the hall. He fell on his knees before Mary to pour out his tale. It appeared that Sir Henry Jerningham had managed to persuade Northumberland's sailors, lying off Yarmouth to prevent Mary's escaping to the Continent, to defect and join Mary at Framlingham. Even more important they were bringing with them heavy ordnance from the ships.

Mary turned almost gaily to Sir Anthony and said mischievously, "Order all my available troops to assemble in the courtyard, Sir Anthony, and have my white palfrey saddled and caparisoned. I wish to review my army!"

Fifteen minutes later she was listening to the voices of over three hundred men shouting, "Long live our Good Queen Mary," and "Death to all traitors!" Her palfrey reared at the unaccustomed noise and Mary was forced to make the rounds on foot, but nothing could spoil for her the memory of this, her first demonstration of loyalty.

3

Mary sat in the great hall at Framlingham under a canopy of state which had been hastily erected on the dais. The canopy, though torn and dusty, was richly embroidered with the Norfolk arms and Mary could not forbear to smile at this somewhat incongruous note. It was like wearing somebody else's clothes. But she did not smile as the envoys from the Privy Council, who had ridden all the way from London, entered the hall and advancing towards the dais made their obeisances to her. She stared glassily over their heads at the musicians' gallery, with its dark oak panels and ball-flower carving, while the earls of Bedford, Arundel, Shrewsbury, Worcester and Pembroke, the latter but lately married to Jane Dudley's sister Catherine, stood before her shuffling their feet. A little apart from the rest stood Lord Chancellor Rich with his friend William Paget, the late King's Comptroller, and a recently appointed member of the Privy Council.

The silence lengthened. Mary, who was fighting to control her anger, shifted her gaze to the bowed heads before her. Then she noticed the busy, nervous hands plucking at doublet fronts and all at once her anger dissolved like snow in April. Impulsively, she stepped down from the dais and went to stand before the Earl of Arundel. All the men regarded her with startled expressions on their faces and Shrewsbury looked as though he were about to faint. "Arundel," said Mary gently, questioningly, "you and yours were always wont to keep faith with the Tudors and we with you."

Tears streamed down Arundel's face as he knelt before her, face uplifted in urgent appeal, "And will from henceforth, your grace," he promised fervently, trying to keep the shake out of his voice, "or else shall my life answer for it."

"And mine! And mine!" Their voices rang through the hall. Easily moved, Mary brushed a tear from her eye and returned to the dais. She beckoned the earls nearer and they came eagerly. "Are all the rebels taken?" she asked.

"Yes, Madam," confirmed Arundel confidently. "I took Northumberland myself. He had got as far as Cambridge when he heard that he had lost all support. He proclaimed Your Majesty in the market-place there and then surrendered himself to me. I escorted him to London and saw him safe lodged in the Tower. It would have done your heart good, Madam, to see how the traitor was pelted with refuse by the London mob."

"No, my lord, it would not," Mary rebuked him softly and he reddened.

Shrewsbury stepped forward. He was a crooked, dark man, malformed since birth, but a good fighter none the less. He bowed before saying, "Suffolk is in the Tower." He referred to Henry Grey, Marquis of Dorset. The old Duke of Suffolk, Charles Brandon, had died in 1545 and lacking heirs male the title had been offered to his son-in-law, the father of Jane Grey. Suffolk had somewhat naturally supported Northumberland's daring coup.

"And what of the Lady Jane Dudley?" asked Mary.

"She is lodged there too," said Arundel. He dabbed at the tears which still clung to his large, blotchy face with the sleeve of his doublet. Mary smiled at him. "She had no part in the plot, I'll wager," she said.

"No, Madam, I think not," replied Arundel. "The first

she knew of it was when her father took her to the Tower and told her she was to be Queen. The poor child sat for nine days under her canopy of state while Northumberland's supporters came to do her homage and then, when all was over, her father came to tell her that it was time to put off royal state and tore down the canopy over her head."

"No longer the time to dance," murmured Mary.

"What said your grace?"

"Nothing of importance," answered Mary, but she was remembering Catherine Howard. She shook herself slightly to dispel these gloomy thoughts and said briskly, "Well-a-day, my lords, and so God has chosen me as His instrument to restore England to the Church of Rome. His ways are indeed mysterious are they not?"

The earls exchanged stunned glances which Mary misconstrued as awe. She rose. "Come, my lords," she said, "attend me to the chapel. I have given orders for the Rood screen to be set back in its rightful place and long to see it."

The Earl of Bedford mumbled in his beard and trembled for his sweet Abbey of Woburn. He hoped the new Queen was not going to get any peculiar ideas about returning confiscated abbey lands!

4

The road to London was crowded with people to see the Queen come by. The royal procession wound its slow, meandering way from Framlingham to Ipswich, Stratford St. Mary and Colchester. On the fourth day it arrived at Newhall Manor, a place of many memories for Mary. There, representatives of the City of London came to see her to present her with a purple velvet purse containing five hundred crowns in gold. Then the procession was off again, along the road towards London. The crowds thickened, giving joyous tongue to acclaim her presence among them, their rightful Queen, old Harry's daughter, and as like him as a twin pea in a pod. Peeresses of the realm streamed through the Aldgate and out on to the Colchester road, attired in their finest gowns and wearing almost every article of jewellery they possessed. They formed a bright ribbon of colour as they rode along on gaily caparisoned horses with a bevy of squires, pages and barking dogs in attendance.

Five miles from London the royal procession was met by another from Hatfield in the midst of which was the Lady

Elizabeth attired in green and white satin and looking her radiant best. Elizabeth was now twenty years old and although she could not, even in the widest sense, be termed beautiful, there was a delicate, waif-like quality about her, an exquisite femininity which brought out the protective instinct in the male sex and caused the watching crowds to gape with admiration. Her white, almost transparent complexion, formed a pleasing contrast to her light red hair and her dark grey, near violet eyes. Her mouth, like Mary's, was small but without the other's primness.

Mary greeted her sister coolly. It was five years since she had last seen her and she remembered how annoyed she had been to find that the fifteen-year-old girl had become infected with the ideas and precepts of the Reformers. She had remonstrated with Elizabeth at the time for reading heretical books and Elizabeth had accepted the rebuke with characteristic imperturbability, eyes lowered to conceal her real thoughts, one long finger marking her place in Nicholas Udall's *Flowers for Latin Spekynge.* She had continued to read the books and Mary had no power to stop her. Mary had felt sorely disappointed that the lovely, bouncing child with whom she had played in the nurseries at Hatfield and Eltham had turned into this self-sufficient, rather calculating young person.

The sisters dismounted and exchanged sterile kisses while the crowds, held at bay by the household guard, watched with eager curiosity this interesting reunion. "You are looking marvellous well, sister," remarked Mary stiffly. "I swear your gown makes mine look quite shabby." She had not meant to voice this envious thought and could have bitten out her tongue as she saw the slow, satisfied smile which spread across Elizabeth's pale features. It was quickly gone to be replaced by a more decorous expression. "May I offer your my felicitations, your grace, on your deliverance from the hands of the rebels?"

Mary acknowledged the compliment graciously. "I owe my life to Sir Thomas Throckmorton," she said. "I shall not forget him. It was fortunate, sister, that that vile wretch Northumberland did not send you a like summons to come to court. You might have fared ill at his hands."

"The duke sent me a summons," replied Elizabeth gravely, "but I felt uneasy and forbore to make the journey." The same pleased smile illuminated her features. It irritated Mary into retorting, "Wise of you, sister, to consider the

safety of your own person before the needs of a sick child."
Elizabeth blinked and was silent.

The two women remounted, assisted by willing, helpful hands, and the unwieldy company proceeded on its way. Sir Edward Waldegrave advised Mary to lodge without the city walls that night so that she might make her progress to the Tower new-clothed and refreshed. Thankfully she agreed and arrangements were made for her and her ladies to stay the night at the Earl of Shrewsbury's house, just without the city.

New-clothed, she thought wryly, as she sat in her temporary lodgings. I have no new clothes. Suddenly she felt she could not bear the idea of riding through London, bowing to a curious populace in a worn dress, with Elizabeth riding beside her resplendent in white and green satin.

She took counsel with Jane Dormer and Susan Clarencieux. "I have no money until I get to the Tower," she sighed, "and anyway there is no time. Perhaps I can wear a cloak to hide my old gown."

Jane Dormer was plucking thoughtfully at her bottom lip. "Madam," she said, "I know a dressmaker who lives at Crutched Friars within the city. She is cousin to my mother and keeps in her establishment good supplies of cloth, for she serves I believe many ladies of the court. If you will give me leave to go I am sure that something can be arranged."

Mary's face lit up. "Oh Jane, think you she would work all night for me?"

"I'd take an oath on it, Madam. They say the citizens are wild with joy at your coming. Mistress Kersey will be only too glad of the opportunity to serve you."

Mary became quite excited at the prospect of a new gown. "Purple velvet, Jane, if she has it," she said, "and silver brocade for the under-gown. Do you think she can manage a hood?"

"Surely."

"Then let it be made of the same purple velvet and sewn with silver bands. Oh heavens!" she slapped her forehead and moaned. "Jewels! I have no jewels save my diamond ring and my mother's gold cross." Mary was unable to keep a note of envy from creeping into her voice as she added, "Did you see that necklace my sister was wearing? Jesu alone knows where she got it. She is supposed to have been in worse case than me all these years."

"Some gentleman perhaps, Madam?" suggested Susan Clarencieux.

Mary laughed. "Yes," she agreed, "most like."

Jane Dormer remained silent. She had recognised Elizabeth's ruby necklace as being one that had once belonged to Queen Catherine Parr. Doubtless the gentleman had been Thomas Seymour.

The ladies were taking Mary's measurements when there was a knock on the chamber door and a page entered to announce that the Lady Anne of Cleves had come to pay her respects to her grace.

Mary beamed. "Show her in, Edward," she commanded. "I shall be right glad to see her." Mary did not know Anne of Cleves well, but she considered that she had been shamefully ill-used by her father and had accepted her banishment with extraordinary dignity. Mary was used to being humiliated herself and she could understand how Anne must have felt.

A very stout lady appeared in the doorway and curtsying with great care advanced to kiss Mary's hand. "My felicitations to your grace," she said in her thick Flemish accent. "How like you are to your father."

Mary smiled. "So I have been told." She surveyed the short, plump figure before her. Anne was dressed in the Flemish style in a gown of bright saffron yellow with silver brocade sleeves, puffed and banded. The bodice of the gown was richly embroidered and sewn with seed pearls, rubies and emeralds. Anne's blonde head was encased in a tight-fitting coif of stiffened white lawn and round her neck hung a magnificent necklace of goldsmiths' work set with diamonds, rubies and sapphires.

Mary was dazzled by this colourful display. Her eyes fastened on the necklace which had been part of Anne's "pay-off" from King Henry. Following the direction of her glance Anne queried smiling, "You like?"

Mary's voice was weak. "Very much."

"You shall have it then," pronounced Anne. "This shall be my Coronation gift to Your Majesty." So saying she removed the costly ornament and handed it to Mary who gaped at it disbelievingly. "But, my lady. You are much too generous. I cannot take . . ."

"Her grace was just saying," put in Jane Dormer swiftly, "that she has no jewels to wear for the procession through London tomorrow. Your gift is timely, my lady."

"Ach, so?" Anne raised pudgy hands in a gesture of distress. Her fat pudding face, with the round blue doll's eyes was all concern. "I shall send immediately to my lodgings and tell one of my ladies to bring for your grace my box of jewels. It shall be at your disposal, Madam."

"I shall return them as soon as I reach the Tower," Mary promised her gratefully. Anne nodded and smiled, pleased that she had been able to help this lady who, like herself, had once been cast shamefully aside. "As your grace pleases," she said.

5

After they had all left her for the night and Susan and Jane had ensconced themselves in the adjoining chamber, Mary climbed out of bed, and carrying the single candle to the wall mirror, gazed long on her reflection. She saw a middle-aged woman of thirty-seven who looked forty-seven. The red-gold hair was still as bright and as abundant as before and the eyes looked the same, being curiously childlike and innocent, but the face was prematurely lined. Deep furrows marked her brow and traced a path from nose to mouth. The thin skin round her eyes was criss-crossed with tiny lines and already unsightly wrinkles were beginning to form. Ah God, she looked old. In the last few days her mind had turned more and more to the question of marriage. She could not rule alone, that much was certain. It was unheard of for a woman to reign without a man at her side, in England anyway. The only time it had been tried, long years ago, it had ended in disaster and civil war. But whom could she marry? There were not many elderly, eligible princes in Europe. Only . . . But no, she must not even think it, for he who was uppermost in her mind was nine years younger than herself, not elderly at all. All the same, as she crept back to bed and pulled the covers to her chin, the name would keep repeating itself. She fell asleep with it on her lips.

6

So Mary rode through London richly clad after all and the willing dressmaker had even managed to supply a train of the same material as the gown, which was proudly held by Sir Anthony Browne. The royal procession had skirted London to enter by the New Gate so that all the citizens could have a sight of their new sovereign. The shouts of the crowd nearly deafened Mary and she marvelled at the ingenuity of some of the tableaux and pageants which had been prepared against her coming. Gold angels blew silver trumpets high above her head and the red dragon of Wales breathed real fire from his nostrils. A huge Beaufort portcullis, made out of silver-painted wood, was lowered in the path of the procession and then raised to reveal twelve maidens covered from head to toe in red and white Tudor roses. They chanted complimentary verses at Mary in very bad Latin and she laughed delightedly. By the time she reached Cheapside she had been presented with twelve purses full of gold crowns, enough and much more to pay for her fine new gown! She thought sadly of Edward as she clutched the purses to her and remembered that he had found the weight of a single one too heavy.

She was quite tired by the time the gates of the Tower came into view and the old familiar light-headed sensation which presaged a headache came upon her. At the Byward Tower she was met by the Constable and the Lieutenant, Sir John Bridges, and behind them she saw four kneeling figures. There was Norfolk, looking so old that she scarce recognised him. Beside him was Stephen Gardiner, Bishop of Winchester and Bishop Bonner of London and at the end of the line young Edward Courtenay who had been imprisoned since he was a youth and had grown up in the Tower. She raised each of them individually and kissed them on the cheek, then turning to the Lieutenant said, "These are my prisoners, Sir John. I am taking them out of your keeping." Sir John bowed and smiled broadly and the four men followed Mary into the Tower. As she passed the gaoler's house she chanced to look up and was startled to see framed in the casement a small, wan face. It was the Lady Jane Dudley.

HAMPTON COURT

October, 1553

I

Elizabeth looked sullenly at Susan Clarencieux and said rebelliously, "What does she want now?"

Susan's usually kind face was sternly disapproving. "Her grace," she said, pointedly emphasising Mary's title, "wishes to speak with you in her bedchamber."

"Now?" This with an exaggerated sigh of resignation.

"At once!" Susan replied sharply.

There was no help for it. Elizabeth put down the book she had been reading and signed to her lady-in-waiting, Catherine Ashley, to bring her hood. Elizabeth never wore her hood within doors if she could help it. She hated the feel of its constricting hold on her head.

Catherine Ashley, plump and dark, with brilliant colouring, was more than a lady-in-waiting. She had been with Elizabeth for fifteen years, her closest and most intimate friend. She brought the hood and placed it on her mistress's head, carefully arranging the pleats of the stiffened flap. Susan Clarencieux was still waiting and Elizabeth said shortly, "Go you on, Mistress Clarencieux. I will follow directly." She did not want to be shepherded to Mary's bedchamber like a wanton, misbehaving child.

Susan bowed her head and withdrew and as soon as Elizabeth judged her to be out of earshot she gave vent to a harsh, restricted scream through tightly clenched teeth. "She is going to pester me again about my religion. I know it," she said.

Catherine's red-cheeked face expressed sympathy. "You could appear to agree with her grace," she suggested.

"Mmm," replied Elizabeth thoughtfully, "but 'tis the principle of the thing, Kate. She is so sure she is right. One would think God Himself had spoken to her. She will see no other point of view save her own. There is a fanatical light in her eyes when she speaks of her religion which I like not. Extremists bore me."

"If you do not wish to incur her grace's displeasure you

will make pretence of agreeing with her," insisted Catherine wisely. "If I know you, my lady, I warrant you are not so set on the reformed religion that you would not change it for expedience's sake."

Elizabeth laughed. "You know me, Kate," she conceded. She heaved a deep sigh. "I'd better go. Send for my bear-ward while I am gone and arrange a bear-baiting in the clock court tonight, for I warn you my mood will be savage when I return."

Elizabeth found her sister seated at a small table in her bedchamber with an open Bible before her, Jerome's Vulgate version, of course. Beside the Bible lay a bundle of yellowing parchments tied together with a green ribbon. Elizabeth looked at the latter incuriously. She sensed at once that Mary was not in the best of humours. The Queen kept rubbing her right temple, a sure sign that she had one of her headaches. She glanced up quickly as Elizabeth entered and curtsied to her, and began without preamble to question her. "Have you thought, sister, about our last discussion on the matter of images?"

"Yes, Madam," replied Elizabeth gravely, eyes downcast, "and I am still of the opinion that they are unnecessary for the true worship of God."

"Are you so?" Once more Mary's hand reached for her temple. She stared hostilely at her sister. Elizabeth just stood there, meek as a mouse, defying her with her smooth tongue and decorous, calculated silences. Well, this time she might be in for a shock. Mary picked up the bundle of parchments on her table and untied the ribbon, wondering at the same time how to go about the business of putting a scare into Elizabeth.

She had been Queen now for three months and during that time she had been so busy about the appointment of new ministers and the punishing of the rebels that she had had no time to think about the matter of religion. She had appointed Stephen Gardiner as her Chancellor and he was supported by a Privy Council composed of the earls of Shrewsbury, Arundel and Derby, the Marquis of Winchester and William Paget. Lord Rich, whom she detested, she had dismissed altogether.

For many weeks she had sat closeted with these men, day after weary day, night after weary night, sorting out the chaotic mess left over from her brother's reign which had been no reign at all really, merely a juggling for power by avaricious men who had used a young, inexperienced boy as a screen for their ambitions.

As to the rebels, Mary had been inclined towards leniency with them and only Northumberland and his two principal supporters, Sir John Gates and Sir Thomas Palmer, had been executed. Suffolk she had freed on the plea of his wife, Frances Brandon, her cousin, and the Lady Jane Dudley and her husband Guilford she intended to keep in the Tower for a while to cool their heels. The new Spanish ambassador, one Simon Renard, who had succeeded Van der Delft in 1552, was aghast at what he considered her idiotic clemency and did not hesitate to tell her so. She had ignored him. She had seen too much bloodshed in her life to want to be the promoter of more.

Inevitably, now that things had calmed down a little, her mind had turned to the subject of religion and she had begun to examine a small, niggling doubt which had formed in the back of her mind soon after her accession. Confident at first that she had only to say the word to bring England back to the feet of Rome, she had been astonished and incredibly disappointed when Gardiner advised her to stay her hand until "things had settled down". In the matter of her brother's burial, which she had wanted conducted with all the rites of the Catholic Church, her Chancellor had decreed that the ceremony should be in accordance with the rites of the Protestant Church with Thomas Cranmer, who was after all, still Archbishop of Canterbury, officiating. She might, if she wished hold a Requiem Mass for her brother in the privacy of her own chapel. There had been yet another shock in store for her when she discovered that her cousin the Emperor was detaining Reginald Pole in Brussels because he feared that Pole, now in Holy orders and a Cardinal to boot, would interfere too arbitrarily in religious affairs.

"But the people want to return to the Church of Rome," Mary had protested to Gardiner. "'Twas only the wickedness of the ministers in my brother's reign which forced the New Faith upon them." Gardiner had not disillusioned her. Had not told her that many were now Protestant from choice and many more enjoying the benefits of confiscated abbey lands which they would be loath to give up. Mary had puzzled over the matter until her head whirled, but she could find no answer to the apparent mystery and now there was talk of disturbances at her forthcoming Coronation. Cranmer had spoken out against the Mass and although he had immediately been clapped into prison for his pains the damage had been done. And what about the chrism for her Coronation? Oil hallowed in England, still under the Pope's ban of excommunication, was not hallowed at all. She would have to send to the Pope for absolution and ask him for some oil hallowed in Rome. The pulse in her head throbbed with dull, clunking beats. Her period was late again and she was feeling like an overstuffed bolster. Elizabeth was still standing before her unmoving, her beautiful hands gracefully linked. Mary shuffled the parchments unnecessarily. "Do you know what I have here, sister?"

The bowed head was raised and the dark grey eyes politely inquiring. "No, your grace."

"These, sister, are the old heresy laws passed during the reign of my ancestor Henry the Fourth when the Lollards were so troublesome. Do you know what the penalty for heresy was, sister?"

Elizabeth did know but she said nothing. The words "my ancestor" rang in her ears. Henry the Fourth was her ancestor too. Was Mary denying their shared relationship to him? An uncomfortable lump formed in her throat. Her fingers moved restlessly.

"Burning at the stake!" Mary was declaiming dramatically, her deep voice, now almost as rough as a man's, filling the bedchamber.

Small beads of perspiration appeared on Elizabeth's brow. "Lollards, Madam," she said breathlessly, "they were quite different. I mean they even denied . . ."

"Heretics are heretics," boomed Mary. "Anyone who denies even the lesser of the ancient rites of the Catholic Church to be God's divine law are guilty of heresy."

"I . . . I . . . do not deny . . . what I should say is I . . ." Mary interrupted her again. "You believe that the daily sacrifice of the Mass is a repetition of the sacrifice of the Cross and a renewal of Christ's sufferings?"

Elizabeth hesitated for the fraction of a second before answering boldly, "No, Madam, I do not. Our Blessed Lord's sufferings took place once for all at Calvary and cannot be repeated. It was a full and perfect sacrifice and atoned for the sins of the whole world for ever. When we partake of the bread and wine we do it in remembrance only of that sacrifice."

She had gone too far. It was unlike her thus to show her hand, but her sister's bullying had weakened her ability to dissemble. She knew she would have to back down. Mary's face was like thunder. In that moment her resemblance to her father was striking. Elizabeth trembled.

"You do not believe then that it is Christ's Body that enters yours at the communion, His Blood that you drink?" rasped Mary. She was clenching and unclenching her hands with savage rapidity, leaving little crescent-shaped indentations on her palms.

Elizabeth decided on immediate capitulation. "I should like to believe that the bread and wine are transformed at the moment of communion, your grace," she said dully. "Perhaps I have been in grave error all these years. My tutors you understand were all of the New Faith. I have been instructed in the ways of the reformers from a very early age." The dark grey eyes were begging now for understanding.

Mary ignored their plea. "Then you will not object to attending Mass?"

"No, your grace."

It was over. Mary, who so often before had been bullied into submission, was wise in the ways of tormentors. She began to re-tie the parchments saying cheerfully, "'Tis the anniversary of poor Edward's birth three days hence. How pleasant it would be if you came to Mass on that day. You will, meanwhile, have ample time to meditate on what I have said during our little conversations and get yourself into the right frame of mind. Promise me now that you will spend the next two nights in prayer and meditation?"

"I promise, your grace." Elizabeth's face was a stony, rebellious mask.

"You may go now." Mary turned a dismissive back on her sister.

Elizabeth curtsied and would have stuck out her tongue had not Susan Clarencieux and Jane Dormer, those two old harpies as she called them, been watching her from their stations by the window. With a flirt of her green velvet skirt she was gone.

2

On the anniversary of Edward's birthday Mary dressed carefully for Mass. She felt keenly the significance of the occasion. Elizabeth, brought up on the teachings of the Reformers, in the same manner as her brother Edward, had seldom been to Mass. Mary was sure that once she started attending regularly again she would forget all that Protestant vileness, instilled into her for years, and be so enthralled by the mystery of the Real Presence that she would be a good Catholic ever afterwards. The Queen's naîvety, at the advanced age of thirty-seven, was something even her closest friends marvelled at but did not admire.

Mary was surprised and a little annoyed to find that Elizabeth had not yet come to the chapel. She had expected that for courtesy's sake she would be there first. The chaplain was ready to begin the introit and looked at her for a sign. Mary looked about her. The chapel was full this morning, word having got round that the Lady Elizabeth, a self-confessed adherent of the New Faith, was going to Mass. Behind his hand Shrewsbury whispered to Arundel that it was just like the Lady Elizabeth to keep them all waiting, the proud-stomached brat. "She's a Tudor right enough," agreed Arundel.

Meanwhile, Mary had no intention of keeping everyone waiting indefinitely for Elizabeth, so she sent Susan Clarencieux to find her. Susan returned within five minutes bearing the information that the Lady Elizabeth was suffering from cramps in the stomach and begged to be excused. Mary was so angry that for the first time in her life she forgot to look at the Host during the elevation.

After the ceremony was over she stormed off to Elizabeth's apartments, followed by her ladies, and pushing the startled Catherine Ashley aside with a sweeping movement of her hand, confronted Elizabeth who was reclining palely on a couch, a cup of wine at her side and one hand delicately spread across her abdomen. "How now, Madam!" she snapped, "a goodly start you have made to your soul's benefit. I warrant that 'twould take more than a belly cramp to keep me from my dutiful worship of God."

Elizabeth closed her eyes and murmured, "My stomach pains me sore, your grace, and . . . and I . . . I think that I need more instruction before I shall be fit to go to Mass. There are certain points upon which my mind is still hazy."

"I marvel not at all that your mind is hazy, sister, since you are surrounded by Protestant ditherers." Here Mary shot a venomous look at Catherine Ashley who rudely tried to outstare her.

"If I could but have a little more time, your grace," pleaded Elizabeth weakly.

"Time! Time you want is it? You have had time a-plenty. Time which you could have spent more profitably. When you were busy seducing Thomas Seymour you had a deal of time . . ."

Elizabeth's eyes snapped open. This was the first time Mary had ever made reference to the Seymour episode. She had thought her ignorant of it.

"Aha!" Mary's tone was triumphant. "That surprises your ladyship does it not? Think not to keep that little business close, sister, for all the world knows of it."

Mary's anger had exhausted her and she felt drained. She turned to leave, but could not resist a parting shot. "What can one expect," she asked of the empty air, "from the daughter of a musician and a whore?" She found the shocked silence which followed her remark as satisfying as she could have wished.

3

That same evening the Queen sent for Simon Renard, the Spanish ambassador. She had done a great deal of thinking during the day as she sat in Council and signed their interminable papers. Her thoughts, sometimes confused, sometimes brilliantly clear, had led her to one conclusion. She must marry in the hope that she could bear a child if Elizabeth were not to succeed her to the throne. So she sent for Simon Renard because in so important a matter she must have the advice of Spain and because she hoped he would suggest as a possible husband for her the one person who had been in her mind for a long time.

Renard came, a small, dark figure in black velvet, deep-browed and long-nosed with soulful brown eyes, their look of compassion belied by a fiercely determined and cruel mouth.

To her surprise Mary found it difficult to broach the subject of marriage and she exchanged generalities with the ambassador until Renard's glance became curious and his brown eyes alert. When Mary was left with nothing save the English climate to discuss she took the plunge. "Messire Renard," she began, her brow creased with anxiety. "I think 'twould be politic for me to marry. I must warn you, however, that my Council are not whole-heartedly in agreement with me over this. Gardiner seems to think that I am too old and past the time when I could safely bear a child." She fixed Renard with a stare which defied him to agree with this unflattering opinion.

"Doubtless your ministers fear that marriage and affairs of state would be too much for a gently reared lady, your grace." replied Renard diplomatically, "but I think they misjudge you, for in my opinon you are quite capable of coping with both."

Mary smiled with gratification. "You think then that I should marry, Messire?"

"Of a surety, your grace. How else is the realm to be restored to the Church of Rome? If the Lady Elizabeth who is, forgive me, tending towards the reformed religion, should succeed you, I fear for the future of the realm. Were your grave to give England a male heir, however . . ."

"The Lady Elizabeth is a bastard." Mary spoke tersely.

"She can be legitimised, as was Your Majesty, by Act of Parliament."

"Messire Renard, I was never a bastard," protested Mary hotly and her cheeks reddened as they always did when this term was applied to her, however indirectly.

"Of course, your grace was not," soothed Renard. "I did not mean to suggest any such thing. I was merely pointing out that your English Parliament does not seem to baulk at passing an Act one minute and revoking it the next as the mood suits them."

Mary fell silent. She knew perfectly well that Elizabeth was her father's daughter and her own half-sister and that she would succeed her in due course of time if she did not marry and bear a child. She still clung stubbornly to the idea that Elizabeth might be Mark Smeaton's child but she did not really believe it. It was just that if you thought about something long enough you could eventually come to believe that it was so. And even though Elizabeth was still officially a bastard, her father's marriage to Anne Boleyn having been declared invalid by the ever-obliging Cranmer, Renard was right when he said that this situation could be reversed in the twinkling of an eye.

The silence lengthened uncomfortably. Mary was the first to break it. "If I were to marry, Messire, whom would you suggest?"

Renard appeared to consider the problem, pulling at his neat, tightly curling beard. "Er . . . perhaps young Edward Courtenay, your grace's cousin . . . ?"

"I do not know him well enough. I think I should marry

abroad," replied Mary swiftly, annoyed by Renard's apparent obtuseness. Surely he must know whom she had in mind? He did, but he had received strict orders from the Emperor Charles that the suggestion to marry his son Philip must come from the Queen herself.

Mary tried again. "I cannot think of one eligible prince," she said and forced a laugh.

Casually, Renard steered her in the right direction. "Your grace would not contemplate marrying a widower?"

"I might," said Mary quickly. Philip was a widower.

"A widower of say perhaps twenty-eight or -nine would not be too young for your grace?"

"Philip of Spain is twenty-eight," said Mary before she could stop herself.

It was out.

Renard smiled benevolently. Within minutes the matter was settled and he had agreed to make the first approach to the Emperor, a mere formality, of course. The Emperor, Renard assured Mary, would be delighted. They went on to discuss other subjects with greater ease, but first Mary warned Renard to say nothing of the marriage project to Antoine de Noailles, the French ambassador. She wanted no interference from King Henri of France. She confided to the ambassador her worry about the English people's reluctance to return to the Roman fold. "Protestantism has a bigger hold than I had at first thought," she said.

"Stronger measures may be necessary to deal with heretics," hinted Renard darkly.

"Stronger measures, Messire?"

"If need be, your grace, they must be taught a salutary lesson."

"What mean you?"

"Why, burning at the stake is the only remedy for heretics."

"Oh no, I could not countenance that, Messire!" Mary was horrified. "I want no persecution in my reign." She thought about the old heresy laws which she had used to frighten Elizabeth. She was already feeling a little ashamed of herself for having used such methods with her sister. All the same this sort of threat might serve to deter those more hardened heretics who seemed bent on the destruction of their souls. Threats could do no harm. But she wanted no burnings.

Wisely, Renard dropped the subject—for the moment. He

was surprised and not a little embarrassed by Mary's next question. "Messire, tell me, is Philip handsome?" She was watching him eagerly and Renard detected a certain coyness in her manner which sat ill upon this small, middle-aged creature. He smiled at her. "I will arrange for his portrait to be sent to your grace. Then may you judge for yourself."

Mary clapped her hands together childishly. "Oh, Messire, how good of you. I should like that well."

The interview was at an end and Renard was bowing himself out when Mary called after him, "Messire, you do not think I am too old to bear a child?"

Renard blinked. For once he was almost at a loss. "N . . . no, your grace. I am sure your grace will present the realm with a fine son in God's good time." Sweating, he made his escape.

Mary gazed sadly after him. How she missed her dear Eustace Chapuys. He would not have lied to her.

LONDON–WINCHESTER

February–July, 1554

I

She went to her crowning apprehensive of demonstrations so that she could not concentrate as hard as she would have wished on the solemnity and ceremonial which encompassed her. She felt slightly ridiculous girded with the great sword of state and with spurs fastened to her heels and was glad when these symbols of sovereignty were removed, to be replaced by the orb and sceptre, the latter containing a piece of the True Cross. But at the High Mass which followed, her mind was all for God and so ecstatic was her face that some thought she spoke with God Himself.

When it was all over she thought perhaps that she had worried overmuch about the unsettled state of the realm, but then the news of her proposed marriage to the Prince of Spain became public knowledge and rebellion was again in the air. The Duke of Suffolk, whom she had mercifully spared after her accession, rode north with his sons to rouse the midlands and Sir Thomas Wyatt, son of the poet Wyatt who had loved Anne Boleyn, mustered his men of Kent at Rochester town and marched on London. Mary stood firm during the crisis even though her life was in danger, Gardiner urged her to leave London and seek refuge farther north, but she would not. Instead she ordered her servants to saddle and caparison her favourite white palfrey and rode down to the Guildhall to deliver a speech to the citizens of London as stirring and courageous as anything her sister was to utter in the far-distant future. She was cheered to the echo and rode calmly back to Westminster to wait for the outcome of the rebellion. That night she would not undress but lay on her great bed with a naked sword at her side. Three days later Wyatt made his move and in a few hours all was over. The attack mercifully failed and Wyatt was captured and taken to the Tower together with his fellow-rebels, such men as the Knevetts, the Isley brothers, Cuthbert Vaughan and many others.

Two days later, in the privacy of her bedchamber, before

her *prie-dieu* hung with cloth of gold and supporting a three-foot high figure of Christ on the cross, she prayed for guidance. Her intended marriage to the Prince of Spain had sparked off a bloody rebellion. Was she, therefore, justified in carrying the proposal to the ultimate? God remaining implacably and unaccountably silent she sent for Simon Renard for earthly counsel. He came, late though the hour was, followed by three of Mary's ladies who cared for her reputation. She sent them away. She had preserved her virtue intact for thirty-eight years. She was not like to lose it now. "The people do not like my proposed marriage to the Prince of Spain," she told Renard harshly. "The late rebellion proves it. I am beginning to doubt the wisdom of it."

Renard was aghast. "Your grace cannot mean that," he said, twisting a button on his doublet. "Why, when the English people see what a sober, kindly prince is Philip they will forget all their doubts. The rebellion is your Chancellor's fault, Madam. He has been too lenient with heretics and trouble-makers."

"On my orders," retorted Mary.

Renard threw his hands wide in a gesture of appeal. "Your grace, have you not seen all the anti-Catholic tracts and pamphlets that are circulating at this very moment, stirring up bloody strife in the realm?"

Mary shook her head disbelievingly, but Renard persisted. "It is so, you make take my word for it, your grace. With Prince Philip at your side, however, these troublesome pamphlets can be suppressed. Heretics will not dare to rear their heads and England will be brought peacefully back to Rome." His persuasive voice droned on and Mary, who wanted nothing more in the world than to be convinced that marriage to Philip was the course God desired for her was convinced, but she was still Queen enough to put her country before her heart. "The prince must not be allowed to interfere in matters of government," she warned Renard, "nor may he put his own people into office. The Council would not allow that."

"Your grace, the prince would not dream of interfering in English affairs," lied Renard.

"Of course, Messire," said Mary, apparently ignoring the assurance and eyeing the ambassador warily, "I know little of the prince. If he wants a passionate, pleasure-loving wife, I am not for him."

"He is sober as a man of fifty," Renard assured her. "As

your grace is aware, he has been married before and has a child. Yet is he virile and will beget children."

Mary blushed and put out a hand to pluck at the crimson hangings of her bed. "I wish I could see him, Messire. You did promise a portrait. If I could but see . . ."

"The portrait is even now on its way to England," Renard broke in swiftly. "'Tis by Tiziano Vercelli who, I have been told, has the prince to the life and dressed in full armour save for his helm. The prince himself insisted that 'twas only fitting that he should be uncovered before the Queen."

Mary smiled for the first time. "I look forward to seeing it, Messire."

Suddenly, Renard moved closer to her and his voice became urgent. "Your grace, before the prince will come into England, before even he will sign the marriage treaty, the rebels must be dealt with."

"Oh, they will be, Messire. They will be," Mary assured him grimly. "If you go about London within the next few days you will see men hanging from every street corner. This time my patience has been tried too far."

"I refer to the ringleaders," insisted the soft voice.

"If you mean Suffolk and his daughter," replied Mary with an air of weariness, "I shall be signing the warrants tomorrow. The Lady Jane Dudley and her husband are to die on the twelfth of this month and Suffolk on the twenty-fourth."

"Wyatt . . ." began Renard.

Annoyed by his persistence and mistaking his meaning, Mary snapped, "Of course Wyatt."

"Wyatt has implicated others," said Renard carefully, finishing what he had been about to say when she had interrupted him.

"Doubtless," said Mary coldly. "Wyatt is a coward. He would not need much racking to confess. There must be a host of accomplices to name, including that knave Throckmorton whom I thought I could trust." Mary had been particularly put out when she found that Nicholas Throckmorton had been one of the conspirators.

"Royal accomplices, too," added Renard significantly.

"Royal accomplices? What mean you, Messire?"

Renard hesitated for a moment but decided to press on. "Wyatt has confessed that the Lady Elizabeth and Edward Courtenay were in the plot and that 'twas planned for them to marry and ascend the throne as joint rulers."

Mary looked stunned. Elizabeth had certainly been in a disgruntled mood after the quarrel about her refusing to come to Mass. Soon after the incident she had asked for and obtained permission to leave court for the manor of Ashridge. "Can this be true?" she whispered.

"On my life."

"A man will say much under torture."

"They were the first names he disclosed." Renard's voice was quietly confident.

"I cannot believe it."

"Wyatt says that Courtenay communicated with the conspirators by cutting a cypher on his lute indicating that he was ready to join them and that the Lady Elizabeth was told by Wyatt to go to Donnington Castle until all was over."

"Why have I not been told all this?" demanded Mary angrily.

"Wyatt's deposition is not yet complete," said Renard. "Your grace will receive a copy when all is known. Meanwhile, I took the liberty of questioning the Chancellor."

"A liberty indeed, Messire," replied Mary sharply. "It would appear that everyone in my court knows what is going on, the while I am left in total ignorance."

Renard was silent and Mary stared at him intently. "What do you expect me to do with the Lady Elizabeth and young Courtenay?"

"What your grace would do with any traitors."

Mary's colour faded. "Oh no, Messire!" she protested.

"At least have them brought to the Tower for questioning," urged Renard. "Your sister, Madam, is greatly to be feared. Make no mistake about it. I believe her to be capable of witchcraft."

"I'll think on it," promised Mary.

2

Elizabeth scratched frantically on the parchment they had given her, watching out of the corner of her eye the bristling figure of William Paulet, Marquis of Winchester. He kept telling her to, "Be yare, yare, lady," but she would not be hurried. She bit the end of her quill until it disintegrated into wispy fragments and racked her brains for something more to say to Mary. Frowning, she read what she had written so far—

'The Lady Elizabeth to the Queen's Grace—

Without cause proved, I am by your Council from you commanded to go to the Tower, a place more wanted for a false traitor than a true subject. I pray to God I may die the shamefullest death that any ever died if I harbour treacherous thoughts against Your Majesty's person, and to this present hour I protest before God, who shall judge my truth whatsoever malicious tongues shall declare, that I never practised, counselled, nor consented to anything that might be prejudicial to your person any way, or dangerous to the state by any means. And therefore I humbly beseech Your Majesty to let me answer before yourself and not suffer me to trust to your counsellors, yea, and afore I go to the Tower, if that be possible, if not, before I be further condemned. Howbeit, I trust assuredly your highness will give me leave to do it afore I go, that thus shamefully I may not be cried out on, as I now shall be, yea and that without cause ...'

And now what? What more could she say? For once she had completely lost her composure. Now she was nothing more than a thoroughly frightened girl who had been caught up in a wild nightmare maelstrom which threatened to engulf her. The summons to court had come out of a clear blue sky. She had been staying at her country manor of Ashridge and enjoying the particularly mild spring weather with the birds nesting early, which everyone knew presaged a good summer. She had been happy. Far from the court and Mary's continual, pounding questions on religion, always religion. And then, one day, as she returned from the chase with two fat bucks to her credit, the messengers had been waiting for her, noble messengers at that, a fact which she found ominous. The Earl of Sussex and the Marquis of Winchester told her that the Queen desired her presence at court. There were certain questions to be asked concerning Wyatt's rebellion. Only she could answer them. She had fainted then and fallen from her horse and they had carried her limp body down the long avenue of larches to the manor house. Her ladies had clustered about her in a twittering throng, casting reproachful glances at the two lords who had so disturbed their mistress as to make her faint. When Elizabeth came to she had admitted to feeling 'most peculiar' and was conveyed to her bed.

Three days passed and still she would not budge from between the covers. The Marquis of Winchester, a hard man, to whom Elizabeth's fainting spell was only one more piece of evidence pointing to her guilt, lost patience and ordered her ladies to dress her and put her in a litter. She would come to London willy-nilly. He cared not, he said, if she did not live to see the city. His orders were merely to convey her person thence. Wanly she submitted, and dressed in a gown of white satin, her favourite colour, sat propped on green satin pillows and when they would have drawn the curtains of the litter about her she said No, she must have air, but Winchester suspected that she wanted to show herself to the people as she rode to London, and he was right.

They took her to Whitehall, Wolsey's old palace, where the Queen was in residence, and Elizabeth begged to see her sister, but they turned deaf ears to her pleas. She tugged from her finger the ring, set with a ruby, which Mary had given her all those years ago when she was but a child and asked them to give it to the Queen. They did, but Mary, unmoved by this poignant reminder of the child she had loved, still would not see her. So she had waited, locked in her chamber without attendance, until Gardiner and four members of the Privy Council came to question her about the rebellion. They interrogated her for three weeks in gruelling, daily sessions, but could get nothing out of her and only Gardiner suspected that the determinedly cool exterior masked a terrified girl. In the end they left her, after telling her that she was to be conveyed to the Tower. Almost she broke down. Almost. The Earl of Sussex and the Marquis of Winchester were again deputed to be her escort and she begged them to allow her "at least to write to the Queen's grace, my lords. There can be no harm in that." Reluctantly Winchester gave his permission, brought her parchment, ink and quills and she had begun her letter.

Elizabeth stopped nibbling the end of her quill as inspiration came at last. She scribbled on—'Let conscience move your highness to pardon this my boldness . . .' Thus she managed to prolong the writing of the letter for another two hours and since he had granted her permission to write a letter and could not go back on his word Winchester had perforce to wait, chewing at his nails, until she had finished. Elizabeth concluded her letter by writing the last two sentences on a fresh sheet of parchment. This left a large blank space which she filled in with sprawling loops which would prevent anyone with evil intent towards her from adding anything of an incriminatory nature at the end of the letter. At twenty, Elizabeth was wise in the ways of treachery.

She put down her quill at last, flexed her stiff fingers and sighed with relief. She had achieved her object. The barge which was to convey her to the Tower would miss the tide and she would have to remain at Whitehall for another night. What she had hoped to gain by prolonging the writing of the letter she did not know. Perhaps a faint hope still lurked in the furthest recesses of her brain that Mary might yet see her. It remained unfulfilled. The next day the lords, brooking no delay this time, hustled her out of her chamber, down the outside stair to the garden and so to the landing stairs. As she passed through the garden Elizabeth looked up at the windows of Mary's apartments, hoping for a sign that the Queen had relented. There was none, but she thought she caught sight of a red velvet hood, quickly withdrawn from sight. Red was Mary's favourite colour.

3

Philip of Spain shivered and drew his red felt cloak up to his ears. "Jesu, save us, what a climate!" he groaned.

Ruy Gomez, his principal gentleman and most intimate friend, who was riding beside him, could not have agreed more. It had not stopped raining since they had disembarked at Southampton three days before. "My life, Sire," he said, "I hope your welcome at the English court will be warmer than their weather."

Philip grunted. He raised his voice to shout at his Master of the Horse, the Marquis di Feria, riding in front. "Di Feria, ask the Admiral how far to Winchester!"

Di Feria looked back, nodded and spoke to Lord William Howard who had met the Spanish party at Southampton and was accompanying them to Winchester. They consulted briefly, then di Feria reined in his horse and waited for Philip to come up. "Not more than two English miles, Sire," he reported. "Yonder is the spire of the cathedral."

"Thank God for that," said Philip, his eyes following the direction of di Feria's pointing finger, "I am soaked to the skin." He though longingly of his native Valladolid where the hot sun warmed a man through to the very marrow of his bones and melted his cares to insignificance. He wished that his father had not insisted that he go through with this ill-starred marriage. He liked not the idea of bedding with an old woman, for so he regarded Mary, but the call of duty was greater than the call of his own desires, and he was royal enough to know it. Charles wanted England for Spain and it was up to him, Philip, to see that he got it. "I wonder if I can get her with child?" he mused and it was only when Ruy Gomez laughed that he realised he had spoken his thought aloud.

"I'll wager fifty gold ducats on it, Sire," the younger man said with grinning confidence.

Philip smiled grimly. " 'Tis not my virility I am worried about," he said, " 'tis her fertility. She's old meat."

Ruy Gomez agreed with this uncomplimentary opinion but he said thoughtfully, "My grandmother had a child when she was forty, but then she had already borne eleven others so I suppose her case was different."

"It had become a habit," replied Philip smiling. They laughed and set spurs to their tired horses, eager to reach their lodgings.

The Spaniards arrived at Winchester forty minutes later to be met just outside the city by a reception committee consisting of the earls of Arundel, Shrewsbury, Pembroke and Bedford with their attendants. Philip greeted them courteously in Spanish, for he knew no English, and they led him to his apartments in the cathedral deanery.

After he had changed his wet clothes Philip heard Mass in the cathedral and noticed the purple-draped dais before the high altar where his marriage to Mary was to be celebrated on the morrow. The sight of that empty platform with its barrier of red silk rope, made him think of a scaffold. It was an unhappy comparison. Philip nudged Gomez and pointed to the Rood screen which had been torn down at the Reformation and hastily re-positioned after Mary's accession, so that it was no longer in line with the pillars of the chancel arch. "So it is true," he whispered.' 'They actually tore down the Rood screens."

"Es posible?" murmured Gomez. The tremendous religious upheaval which had taken place in England was suddenly borne in upon these men from an alien and staunchly Catholic land.

The Spanish party left the cathedral to partake of a meal in their apartments and then it was time for Philip to dress for his first meeting with Mary. He had chosen to wear black velvet overlaid with silver filigree work and about his neck hung the Order of the Golden Fleece. The ensemble was simple and elegant and despite his somewhat low stature Philip looked royal to the core. He was not strikingly handsome, but his face had a sensual quality which turned female knees to water. Brown eyes, large and wide-set, dominated the rest of his features which consisted of a long, rather flat nose and a wide, loose-lipped mouth. His jutting Habsburg chin sprouted a fine gold beard which was several shades darker than his hair.

Gomez gave Philip's doublet a last tug and stood back admiringly. "Your Highness has never looked so well."

Philip shrugged off the compliment. "I could wish it were for a more auspicious occasion."

"The occasion is auspicious enough," commented Gomez with the privilege of long friendship, " 'tis the bride who is somewhat lacking."

"Her portraits show her passing fair," said Philip hopefully.

Gomez was doubtful. "I had it from the wife of the English ambassador that she is more lined than one would expect for her age, though her hair is a good colour."

"What about her figure?"

"Scrawny I fear, Sire."

"Scrawnee? What sort of word is that?"

"It means very thin," grinned Gomez.

"Madre de Dios," muttered Philip and squared his shoulders. "Who is to go with us to this meeting?" he asked.

"The four English nobles who met us," replied Gomez. "We can take di Feria and Alva if you wish."

"No, no," said Philip, flapping his hand in a dismissive gesture, "Let us not overwhelm them with Spaniards yet. If all goes well they will see more of us anon."

Gomez laughed. "I wonder what the English ladies are like?" he said. "I am told they are not so close guarded as ours."

Philip wagged an admonitory finger at him. "For God's sake, Ruy, don't get any of them with child yet. We must proceed with caution."

"I have only to wink at them to get them with child," boasted Gomez.

Philip roared with laughter, punched his friend playfully in the ribs and bade him summon the English nobles to attend him.

It was almost dark now. The small party, led by the Earl of Bedford, descended an outside stair to the garden and walked across a square of lawn to another outside stair which led to the apartments allotted to the Queen and directly into the Bishop's presence chamber.

Mary was waiting for him attired in black velvet with an undergown of cloth of gold. Her head-tire was of diamonds and rubies and about her neck she wore a magnificent collar of the same. Not all this finery, however, could disguise the fact that she was ageing and even though Philip had expected the worst, he received a small shock at sight of her.

She had been pacing the chamber nervously when she heard his step on the stair and spun round, forcing herself to walk slowly towards him as he entered the chamber. She kissed her own hand and extended it towards him and he bowed over it, brushing it lightly with his lips. Then, taking her by the shoulders he drew her to him and kissed her full on the mouth. Living fire coursed through Mary's body, and she almost swooned with joy. Philip was all that she had expected him to be and more, and she fell in love with him on the instant because this man was the only one in the whole of her life whom she knew she could have. This time her betrothed would not be taken from her because of her father's wavering foreign policy, or because he had tired of yet another wife, or simply because he felt like it. She was sovereign now and it was her will that would be done. She was in love with love.

Before introducing Philip to her ladies Mary led him to the dais whereon two state chairs had been set side by side. Together they mounted the steps and he handed her courteously to her chair before seating himself. She turned towards him and clasping her hands in her lap clenched them fiercely together to still their shaking. "Well met . . . Philip," she said faintly. He smiled at her and she noticed the whiteness of his teeth.

"Well met indeed, Mary," he replied.

She could not think what to say next, but it did not matter because he was telling her, in a mixture of French and Spanish, that his father had made him King of Naples before he sailed for England so that she might marry someone of equal rank with herself; of the vile journey he had had, how rough the sea had been and how he had feared the ship would founder, and then, when they landed, it had been raining and had not stopped since. Was the weather always so terrible in England? He went on to tell her of all the things he had seen along the road from Southampton to Winchester which had caused him to marvel. What was this? What had that been? She was soon happily explaining that in England most churches were built in the Gothic rather than the Byzantine style and that high-born ladies more often travelled on horseback rather than in closed litters, and it was not unusual for them to enter taverns unaccompanied by gentlemen. This last piece of information made him stare at her with raised eyebrows until she was forced to laugh at his wonderment. He laughed too then and soon they were making the ladies and gentlemen break into smiles.

After half an hour's converse Mary decided it was time for introductions and leading Philip from the dais presented first her ladies and then her gentlemen. Philip kissed all the ladies on the mouth, which he had been told was the English fashion, and to her astonishment Mary experienced a pang of jealousy as she saw his eyes devour young Margaret Fitzgerald, a recent addition to her household. Of course the girl was incredibly beautiful. Enough to turn any man's head. She wondered whether to send Margaret to Woodstock where her sister Elizabeth, now released from the Tower, was living under the guardianship of Sir Henry Bedingfield. Instantly, she rebuked herself for such a childish thought.

Philip was asking her if she would teach him how to say good night in English and she mouthed carefully at him, "Good night, my lords and ladies all."

"Good night, my lor-r-rds and ladees ull," he repeated dutifully and everybody clapped. Then he was gone and she was left feeling empty as a discarded wine flagon. Lord William Howard entered into the nuptial spirit and chucking Jane Dormer under the chin said gaily, "And how doth my lusty little brethel?" Jane tried to look shocked, failed miserably and giggled loudly. Mary laughed, too, and turning to Susan Clarencieux repeated Howard's words and gesture in a splendid imitation of the Admiral. Everyone shrieked with laughter, but Susan was horrified. She whispered to Mary, "Madam, a brethel is a whore! My lord Admiral is a light gentleman to talk so." Mary clapped her hand to her mouth and giggled shamefully. How little I know of the ways of the world, she thought. She sobered a little as she realised that she was not quite sure what to expect on her wedding night.

WINDSOR–HAMPTON COURT

August, 1554–May, 1555

I

Mary had not known what to expect on her wedding night, but it was certainly not the quick, painful consummation forced on her by Philip and the abrupt withdrawal from her bed to dice and drink with his gentlemen in the outer chamber. When he left her Mary was desolate. She had been prepared to give him so much love, but he had not asked it of her. She had been humiliated many times in her life and now she knew what it was to be violated. Now had she drunk the cup to the dregs. And yet she loved him and her foolish heart told her that perhaps, in time, he would come to love her in return. Perhaps when she gave him a son. She could not think that so fine a thing could come out of this night's bleak act, but there was always tomorrow and tomorrow.

Her one consolation in the days that followed her marriage was Philip's outward behaviour. His manner to her nobles was exemplary and he gave them no offence, as she had secretly feared he might. The marriage was naturally followed by several weeks of festivities with the court travelling from Winchester to Hampton Court and Greenwich and finishing up at Windsor where Philip was made a Knight of the Garter. Little by little Mary allowed Philip to take over her role on the Council and was instantly rewarded by a more lingering, loving bed-fellow. Joyfully did she succumb to his subtle bribery and allowed him to teach her things which made her blush with shame when the first light of dawn crept through the casements. She blossomed, grew fatter and to crown her new-found happiness her monthly time was late and she believed herself pregnant. She would not believe that this was only the old trouble that had plagued her for years because she had been free of it for a while and besides there were other signs. She was sick in the mornings and her breasts pricked and swelled. Ah, thanks be to Jesu, she was with child. She could not doubt it. She sent for the court midwife, Mistress Blanche Boxley, who examined her carefully, her tiny, rose-bud mouth pursed in concentration. Mary submitted complacently to the painful proddings and when she was done said breathlessly, "Am I with child, Blanche? Tell me quickly."

Mistress Boxley bristled importantly. She coughed to gain time, for, to speak the truth, she was not absolutely certain. All the signs were there to be sure, but in her vast experience Mary's nipples should have darkened and so far they had not.

Mary was watching her intently and Mistress Boxley took a chance. She was almost sure, so what possible harm could there be in telling the Queen what she most wanted to hear? Her small agate eyes twinkled. "Aye, Madam," she said confidently, "you are with child."

Unembarrassedly Mary sank to her knees. "Oh dear Lord, I thank Thee for Thy bountiful mercy," she breathed.

"'Tis a miracle indeed, your grace," responded Mistress Boxley rather tactlessly.

Mary did not care. Nothing could spoil this joyous moment for her. She stood up and began to pace the chamber, a habit of hers when she was violently disturbed or excited. She could not wait to tell Philip. It would be several hours yet before they were alone together. Oh Blessed Virgin, she could not wait that long. She would tell him at the cane game this very forenoon. Mistress Boxley, seeing the Queen's heightened colour delivered a cautionary word. "You must rest, Madam, whenever you can, and remember, 'tis very bad for you and the babe if you get too excited. We have a long way to go yet before the child is safe delivered."

Mary tried to assume her usual decorous expression but without much success. "Oh yes, yes, Blanche, I will remember," she promised with shining eyes. She added gaily, "But may I be permitted to get excited just for today? Just until I tell my dearest lord that I am to bear him a child?"

Mistress Boxley's smile was patronising. These royal ladies. They were all alike. Always so pleased when they found themselves to be with child for the first time, with never a thought to spare for a day, nine months hence, when they'd be writhing in agony and wishing themselves dead. "Just for today, your grace," she agreed.

2

The Spanish cane game was not much to the English taste, but Mary liked it because Philip liked it, and she had therefore arranged to hold one every week for his pleasure. Today it was to take place in the great tiltyard at Windsor. Mary could not wait for the game to begin so that she could tell Philip her wonderful news. As she took her place in the royal stand with her ladies she saw that a sprinkling of English nobles and their wives had assembled in the other stands to watch the performance, but many more were noticeable only by their absence. A sharp stab of irritation marred Mary's happiness in the present moment. Philip was going out of his way to be courteous to her nobles. Why could they not return the compliment? She decided to ask Gardiner to drop a few hints in the right quarter, to the effect that the Queen would appreciate larger audiences at the cane games.

Mary barely had time to seat herself before she was joined by Philip and his gentlemen, among whom was the renowned Duke of Alva, the most hated and feared man in Spain, for he governed his vassals harshly. He bowed ceremoniously to Mary and she gave a little shiver of distaste as he conveyed her hand to his lips. Alva was so very large. Black, oily hair grew in profusion on his enormous head and even the backs of his hands were smothered with dark, curly hairs. The man was predatory, there was no other word to describe him. Alva took his place on the other side of Philip and beyond him sat the Marquis di Feria. Mary noted with amusement the long, languishing glances which he frequently bestowed on Jane Dormer. She wondered how long it would be before di Feria came to ask her for Jane's hand in marriage.

As soon as the royal party were settled in the stand the game began. The minstrels in one of the stands began a march. At the same instant the gates of the tiltyard swung open and two mounted teams rode in side by side and took up their positions facing each other. Each team was brightly apparelled in its own particular 'livery'. Today the prince's men wore green and silver, as a compliment to Mary, and the Duke of Alva's men purple and silver, the duke's own livery. Every man carried a cane about six feet in length. Alva gave the signal and the teams drew apart, wheeling their horses and turning to face each other again in two long lines. Again Alva raised and lowered his arm and the riders charged, the object being to tilt at your opposite number in the 'enemy' line and endeavour to unhorse him. Once unhorsed a man was not allowed to remount and the game went on until all but one were eliminated. It was dull sport to the English who preferred the rough and tumble of the joust and they thought the continuous musical accompaniment effeminate.

Philip was shouting his side on but he could not outshout Alva whose deep baying voice roared forth at regular intervals. Mary cast a sidelong glance at her husband. He seemed to be totally absorbed in watching the contest and she hesitated to divert his attention. So she waited a little and then, during a pause in the game, when a fallen man was being carried away, she leaned towards him, clasped him about the arm and whispered in his ear, "Philip, my beloved, I am with child."

Philip was so surprised that he nearly fell off his seat. He was also a little annoyed that Mary should have chosen this particular time to tell him such tidings. It would have been more fitting if she had waited until they were in the privacy of their own bedchamber. Mary should have known enough of Spanish customs to be aware of this. His annoyance gave place to amusement as he reflected that Ruy Gomez had won his bet. Gomez had put up one hundred ducats to say that Philip would get Mary with child within two months. After seeing his bride Philip had been doubtful. Confidently he had taken Gomez on and now he owed him a hundred ducats. God's blood what a triumph! He had thought her sterile as an old boot. The implications began to dawn upon him. If Mary gave birth to a boy, England would belong to Spain indeed.

Mary was watching him anxiously. "You are pleased, my lord?" she asked uncertainly, puzzled by the mixture of expressions flitting across his face.

Philip awoke from his day-dream and smiled broadly at her. "I am delighted, my Queen," he assured her.

Mary sighed contentedly. "I am almost completely happy for the first time in my life," she said. "There is just one other thing I would wish for."

"And that is?"

"The return to England of my cousin, Cardinal Reginald Pole."

Philip nodded his emphatic agreement. "'Tis time now that he returned. To help us bring England back to the Church of Rome."

Mary frowned thoughtfully. "I fear 'tis the Emperor who still prevents his coming," she said. "He is apprehensive that Reginald will move too fast in the matter of religion and cause disturbances to take place."

Philip laughed. "Father was always over-cautious," he said. "I shall deal with him." He squeezed her hand where it lay on his arm. "When do you expect our child to be born?"

Mary blushed and cast down her eyes. Philip thought she looked slightly ridiculous. He experienced a momentary distaste for her. She was behaving like a green young wife of fifteen. Shyly Mary looked up. "About the beginning of April next year," she said.

"We shall have Pole back ere then," he promised her. She yearned up at him. "I do not know how I managed to deal with affairs of state until your coming, Philip."

Philip grinned to cover his embarrassment. "Men are born to rule, women to breed," he said. Was now a propitious time to broach a matter of some importance? he wondered. He thought so. A woman with child was notably pliant. He said carefully, "There is one thing that I cannot do without *your* help, Mary."

"What is that, beloved?"

"Heretics abound in England," was the sharp rejoinder. "They spring up like weeds. We must take sterner measures with them."

Oh God, here it was again, thought Mary. Sterner measures would have to be taken to stop heresy. How they badgered her. If it was not Philip it was Renard and always they would use the same phrase. Sterner measures. "Already many heretics are imprisoned," she reminded Philip.

"By sterner measures I mean if they persist in their wilful denial of Catholic doctrine they must pay for it with their miserable lives."

One of the prince's team fell off his horse directly in front of Mary. She watched him distractedly as he disentangled his leg from the stirrup and led his horse off the field. "Burning you mean?" she said doubtfully.

"Yes."

"Philip, my dearest, I am sure that such a drastic solution will not be necessary."

"Ah, but it will, my Queen. Naught save the fire will

suppress heresy." Slowly, his hand travelled from her arm to her breast and his fingers sought her nipple under the low-cut bodice. In full view of everyone. Mary shivered with delight and her thighs tingled. She opened her eyes wide to look at him. "Not burning," she pleaded. The teasing hand was swiftly withdrawn from her bodice and Philip turned to smile at Margaret Fitzgerald who sat directly behind Mary. Only a fool could have mistaken his meaning. He had said, plainer than words could express, that either she agreed to his wishes or he would seek diversion elsewhere.

Mary looked miserable and was silent for so long that Philip began to think that his ruse was not working. But she gave in at last. "What must I do?" she asked in a small voice. The hand was returned to her breast and the dark eyes looked deep into hers. "You have only to append your signature to the death warrants I shall give you," Philip told her. "Naught more. There are several noted heretics we know of—in the church of all places. Canker at the heart of religion. They must be cut out." Then, as he saw Mary's worried expression, "They will be given every chance to recant, of course, and admit to the error of their ways. First of all they will be imprisoned and put to the question." Mary shuddered slightly but Philip appeared not to notice. "Only if they remain obdurate will they taste the fire. I shall put Bishop Bonner in charge of the business."

Mary did not answer. A faint echo of her own voice stirred in her memory. "Henceforth, I shall do only what I believe to be right, whatever the cost." Eustace Chapuys had been in no doubt that she had meant what she said. He had not visualised the possibility that she would one day be pliant as wax in the hands of a man who had awakened her physically and aroused all the long-dormant passion of a lusty Tudor. Religious fanatic she certainly was and determined to bring England back to the feet of Rome. Marrying Philip had been one way to ensure that this would be done, but if left to herself she would not have sent men to the fire for their faith. She was trapped by the insistent desires of her body.

Philip was squeezing her breast painfully so that she almost cried out. "There is another, more pleasant favour I have to ask of you, my Queen."

Mary's eyes were glazed with passion. Her body was on fire. She wished she were a serving-wench that she might go behind a hedge with her man for an urgent coupling. As it was she would have to leash her passion until tonight. If only he would not lay his hands on her, all would be well and she would be able to contain herself. If only he would not. Ah God, if only he would. "A favour?" she asked dreamily.

"It is that you bring your sister to court where we can keep an eye on her."

Mary came back to reality with disappointing abruptness. "There's a heretic for you," she sniffed.

"Precisely my point."

"If you insist," she agreed languidly. "She doubtless finds it boring at Woodstock anyway."

Philip smiled. He would know of a way to relieve the Lady Elizabeth's boredom. A cunning, wayward chit if all he heard of her was true. He had not yet been presented to Elizabeth. She had not attended the wedding at Winchester, for she was still virtually a prisoner and under suspicion of having been party to Wyatt's plot to depose Mary. Philip had been thinking for some time now that if Mary died he might yet be able to retain his hold on English affairs by marrying Elizabeth. He removed his hand from his wife's breast and placed it on her thigh. He felt her quiver beneath his touch and permitted himself a small, secret chuckle. She was becoming quite inventive between the sheets this passionate little Tudor of his. He had had many a good laugh about it with Ruy Gomez.

Mary saw his lips curve into a smile and misconstrued it. She leaned more closely towards him. "Have you any more requests beloved?"

God's love, but she was shameless. And at her age, too! Deliberately misunderstanding the arch question Philip said gravely, "Only that you persuade the Council to fix a date for my Coronation."

3

At Hampton Court Mary was awaiting the birth of her child and the fires of Smithfield were already burning. They had been lighted in February, 1555, one John Rogers being the first to be consumed by the flames. He was cheered by the crowd. Many others were to follow after, men such as Bishop Hooper of Gloucester, Bishop Ferrar of St. David's, Bishops Latimer of Worcester and Ridley of London and later Thomas Cranmer. There were others too, men and women of no renown, whose stubborn denial of Catholic doctrine led them to the fire. Bonner did his work well, so well that even Cardinal Pole, now safe returned to England as Papal Legate and installed in Cranmer's See of Canterbury. would have no part of his bloody work. Devout Catholic though he was Pole, like Mary, had contemplated a bloodless return to Rome.

Mary dragged her heavy body down the long gallery, at her side Susan Clarencieux and Jane Dormer. She felt wretchedly ill. It was now the middle of May and her child was long overdue. She had seen her physicians only that morning. They had assured her that she was indeed with child, but that it might not be born until the end of May. Throughout the country prayers were being said in all the parish churches for her safe delivery. Mary saw Gardiner coming towards her. He was limping a little, favouring his right leg, and his head shook ever so slightly. He is getting old she thought. Like me, he is getting old. She pushed the unwelcome reflection to the back of her mind. A woman about to bear a child should not admit to feeling old.

Gardiner bowed and Mary smiled up at him. He said gently, "Your grace, the Lady Elizabeth has been here for a week now. Will you not see her?"

In accordance with Philip's wishes Mary had summoned Elizabeth to court, but when her sister came she had not been able to bring herself to see her. She still suspected her of complicity with Wyatt. She shuddered when she remembered how close she had come to signing a warrant for Elizabeth's execution. Her sister had been so near to death during her three months as a prisoner in the Tower. Elizabeth had known it and requested only that she be dispatched with a sharp sword. But she had had to let her go. She could not have sent her own sister to the block. What though if Elizabeth were not her sister? What if, after all, she was Mark Smeaton's child? The Tudor resemblance could be purely coincidental. There had been talk all those years ago. A deal of talk about Anne Boleyn and that musician of hers who followed her about like a dog and one tale had gained some credence at court. It was to the effect that Mark was wont to hide in a cupboard in the small closet leading off Anne's bedchamber. When she was left alone for the night Anne would call to her old serving-woman for some marmalade and the woman would let Mark out of the cupboard and send him into the Queen. Could it have been so? If only her child would be born. Then it would not matter one way or the other. But if the child died or . . . but she would not let herself pursue that line of thought. Would not face the unpalatable fact that perhaps she was not with child after all. If that were so her reluctant mind demanded, what had made her belly swell, what caused the wretched vomiting?

There was sympathy in Gardiner's faded old eyes as he regarded her. Sympathy and a great, overwhelming pity. Mary hesitated. She would have to see Elizabeth soon. It was stupid and senseless of her to keep putting off the moment and perhaps if she saw her she could remove the mask at last and see into her sister's very soul. Find out the truth about her and Wyatt. It was a well recognised fact that women with child often had second sight. She smiled tiredly at Gardiner. "I will see her tonight after the Vesper hour," she promised. "In my bedchamber."

"I think it would be as well for your grace to do so," replied Gardiner with relief. "I have questioned her yet again about the Wyatt affair but can get nothing out of her. I am inclined now to believe in her innocence."

Mary made no comment on this. "Did Sir Henry Bedingfield bring her to court?" she asked.

Gardiner laughed. "Aye, your grace, and glad enough he was to be relieved of his charge. He says she is a right troublesome minx."

"Poor Sir Henry. I have neglected him. Is he still here?"

"Yes, your grace."

"Tell him I will see him this forenoon to thank him for his good care of the Lady Elizabeth."

"He will be amply rewarded by a sight of your grace's person."

"I doubt it," replied Mary with a touch of humour. "I will see to it that he receives something more tangible."

Gardiner bowed and retired.

That night Elizabeth was brought to Mary's bedchamber by Susan Clarencieux. Mary was seated at a hutch table upon which had been placed her desk box with its hinged lid and book rest. At sight of her sister, Elizabeth rushed towards her and fell to her knees, and without waiting for Mary to say anything began to protest her innocence. Discreetly, on tiptoe, Susan Clarencieux left the sisters together.

"Madam," pleaded Elizabeth with tears in her eyes. "How

can you believe that I would plot to depose you? How can you believe that I would betray my own sister into the hands of those vile rebels?"

Mary's tired eyes searched Elizabeth's face. The girl looked genuinely distressed and yet still the mask was there, concealing the innermost thoughts. "And how am I to believe *you*, Elizabeth?" she said.

"You must believe me, for I speak truth, as God is my judge," was the quiet reply.

"You, to speak of God, Whose commands you disobey every day, persisting as you do in your heresies."

"I am a good Catholic now. I hear Mass twice a day. I have seen the error of my ways." This last was said loudly, and with an air of truculence. Curiously enough the statement did not carry as much conviction as had her quiet denial of complicity in Wyatt's plot.

Mary was too weary to notice such subtleties. With startling suddenness she snapped, "You would have been glad to step into my shoes had Wyatt's plot succeeded and I the victim of an assassin's knife. You and Courtenay, a precious pair to be King and Queen of this realm."

"Madam, I swear I knew naught of any scheme to set me on the throne with Edward Courtenay."

Still Mary was not convinced. "Bedingfield tells me that you scratched two lines of verse on the window-pane of your chamber at Woodstock. 'Much suspected of me, Nothing proved can be'. What did they mean?"

"Exactly what they said. No more, no less."

"They have a certain ambiguity which I like not."

Elizabeth spread wide her arms in a gesture of appeal. "Madam, if my own words cannot convince you of my innocence perhaps those of Courtenay will. When he was questioned on the subject of a possible marriage to me he declared I was of too low birth for him and a bastard into the bargain."

Mary was taken by surprise. She laughed harshly. "There speaks a true Plantagenet."

Elizabeth seized on this sudden lightening of Mary's mood to pluck from her hanging sleeve a set of baby clothes she had herself made for her sister's child. Every article was embroidered with a crooked coronet. Silently, she handed them to Mary who inspected them one by one before laying them gently on her desk box. Despite herself, she was touched, as Elizabeth had known she would be. "I see your needlework does not improve," she commented drily. The eyes of the sisters met. Impulsively, Mary leaned forward and raising Elizabeth to her feet, drew her towards her and kissed her. "I warrant you have been used like others before you," she said. "Go now Elizabeth. I am tired. I shall see you again tomorrow and we can talk together some more. From henceforth you are free of the court."

Was there a gleam of triumph in Elizabeth's eyes? Mary could not be sure. When the girl was gone Philip stepped out from behind the arras. "I think she is innocent," he said thoughtfully.

Mary shrugged. *"Dios sabe,"* she replied wearily.

HAMPTON COURT

August, 1555

1

At Hampton Court the weeks dragged by and still the child was not born. But this self-delusion could not go on much longer. All the quickening signs had ceased, if indeed, they had ever existed outside her heightened imagination, and she must face reality. The court had been so long at Hampton that the palace smelled. She knew it was time to be gone. But still she lingered. Just one more week she told herself and then will I face the truth. Then will I admit before the world that I am not with child. She knew what it was that held her back, prevented her from displaying her usual forthright honesty. Philip was anxious to be gone. He had promised to stay with her at Hampton Court until the child was safely delivered, but of late he had been looking at her with a curious expression in his eyes, half-impatient, half-pitying and he was constantly reminding her that affairs in Flanders needed his attention. His father, he said, was toying with the idea of abdicating and it was vital that he see him to discover his intent. Today he had told her that he would wait four more weeks and then he must be gone whether the child be born or not. She had realised long since, of course, that to him their marriage was one of political expedience only.

Mary wandered round the nursery which had been prepared for the coming of the baby, fingering the cradle and smoothing the satin coverlet embroidered with the Prince of Wales's feathers. So industriously had she and her ladies worked that the nursery contained enough small garments and coverlets to provide for six babies. A tear trickled down her cheek and she wiped it away impatiently. She wished that she had not allowed Philip to persuade her to write to Bishop Bonner telling him that he must be more energetic in his pursuit of heretics. In her opinion Bonner had surpassed himself and surely enough people had gone to the fire already to make other would-be heretics take pause. She began to fear that she had allowed Philip to take too much upon himself. Through him she had given England to Spain. In the days of her youth it had been the English who persecuted her. Perhaps it was not to be wondered at that she had turned to Spain for advice and comfort—to her friend the Emperor. Small wonder too that she had been eager to marry his son.

Her fingers found the stiff, high collar of crown lace which she always wore now to conceal her sagging neck muscles and she tugged at it irritably. She felt stifled. She must get some air. Jane Dormer was sitting by the window of the nursery embroidering yet another cradle cover. Her other ladies were in the adjoining chamber sewing up little bags of lavender and dried herbs to sweeten her clothes chests. She called to Jane. "I think I will take the air in the garden. Summon the other ladies, Jane, and tell them to keep at some little distance from me. I wish to think. I am in no mood for conversation."

Jane Dormer looked at Mary sympathetically and wondered how much longer it would be before the Queen admitted that she was not with child. The whole court had been aware of this depressing fact for three months already and no one had had the courage to tell her, not even the midwife, whose duty it really was.

The day was fair, it being late August, and although the leaves had lost their fresh green colour and had begun to take on the tints of autumn, the air had the wine-like quality of early spring. A day for lovers to wander hand in hand through enchanted gardens. The ladies were glad to be out on such a day and chattered animatedly among themselves. Mary walked rapidly away from them, increasing the distance between until twenty yards separated them. The flowers in the formal beds were full-blown and shedding their petals. They lay in small, untidy heaps on the sanded path under Mary's feet and she scuffed idly at them with the toe of her velvet shoe. She was nearing the knot-garden, came up to it and would have passed on to the sunken garden, when the sound of voices reached her ear and she paused. One of the voices was a man's and it belonged to Philip. There was no mistaking that thick Spanish accent and the curious way he sometimes had of laying emphasis on the last word of every sentence. Mary found herself unashamedly eavesdropping. The temptation to do so was too great and she could not resist it.

Silently she entered the first alley of hedges and stood

stock-still, cocking her ear in the direction of the voices. She could hear a woman's voice now and a look of pain crossed her face. She crept a little farther down the alley and glimpsed a patch of red through the thickly growing leaves of the hedge.

". . . and if I cannot have you, none else shall, my lady, for I swear I will have you locked up in a *convent*."

"Oh Sire, you could not be so cruel!" Mary stiffened. The female voice was that of Margaret Fitzgerald. She cursed herself for a fool. She should have followed her first instinct to send the girl away.

"I could so, my lady," Philip was saying. "How would you like to have your beautiful hair shaved off and that delicious"—he pronounced it 'delisoose'—"white bosom of yours hid beneath drab black *serge*?" His voice deepened and thickened. "Your cheeks are delicate as apple blossom. My hand itches to caress you. Permit me to place it so." There was a suppressed squeal and a giggle and Mary clenched her fists till her nails bit into the flesh of her palms. The thought crossed her mind that Philip's English had improved a great deal in the past few months.

"Become my mistress," Philip urged. "Sail with me to Flanders when this masque here is played out."

"What can your grace mean?" The tone of her voice was arch.

"Come now, lady, you know right well that I refer to the Queen's false pregnancy."

"You do not think she is with child, Sire?"

"Of course I do not, and neither do you."

Margaret Fitzgerald giggled faintly. "Well, we ladies did think that 'twas mighty odd the physicians could not seem to tell her grace exactly when the child was to be born."

Tears streamed down Mary's face now and she doubled up as though in agony. She would have crawled away then save that a third, startled voice exclaimed, "Pardon, Sire, I did not know you were here." It was Ruy Gomez who had apparently come from within the garden.

"What do you here, Ruy?" Philip asked.

"Why, Sire, I fear like yourself I have been engaged in dalliance with a lady. I left her crying into the fountain. I swear if she goes on at this rate we shall all be awash."

"You've got her with child, I suppose," laughed Philip.

"Why no, Sire. That is why she is crying."

All three dissolved into helpless laughter and Mary,

crouching behind the hedge, bit her lip till the blood ran. Philip, when he recovered himself sufficiently, reverted to rapid Spanish. "Ruy, *mi amigo*, now that you are here I would have a moment's speech with you." And in English, "Lady Fitzgerald, I shall see you anon. Wait for me after supper in the blue closet."

There was a rustle of satin brocade and Mary concealed herself quickly in a blind alley at the end of which a stone cupid on a pedestal took aim at unwary lovers. She was only just in time, for a second later Margaret Fitzgerald skipped by her and was gone. Mary wondered what she would think when she came upon the other ladies and was told that the Queen had gone into the garden. She did not care. She stayed where she was, no more able to move than if she had been a fly caught in a spider's web.

Philip was talking to Gomez now. "I must get out of England," he said. "The place suffocates me. My father has a mind to abdicate and there are certain arrangements to be made."

"While the Queen is with child . . ." murmured Gomez.

"The Queen has a tumour in her belly and no one, least of all myself, has the courage to tell her so," retorted Philip.

Mary gasped and placed a hand over her mouth to stifle the cry which rose to her lips.

"The Queen's ladies say she has all the symptoms of pregnancy," replied Gomez.

"All of which can be attributed to something else," said Philip. "She is sick because she has chronic indigestion and her belly swells with the tumour inside it."

Gomez laughed and with the unkindness of youth said, "If she be not pregnant I warrant 'tis through no fault of Your Majesty."

Philip snorted. "I swear she puts my manhood to a severe test. You would not believe Ruy the passion that is stored in that dried-up little woman. When I taught her what it was all about, more to amuse myself than aught else you understand, she became marvellous inventive. I fear if she had not been a Queen she would have been a stewed whore."

"Ah, but whores are more beautiful than her grace," argued Gomez.

"Aye, so they are," agreed Philip ruefully. "The sight of her body, all wrinkled and brown like a walnut, is repellent to say the least."

"It would take God Himself to drink your Majesty's cup."

She could bear no more and wished heartily that she had not stayed to hear so much. Blinded by tears she escaped from the knot-garden. When she returned to her apartments, accompanied by her disturbed, anxious ladies, she wept herself into a severe migraine. Later that day, grey-faced and stony she told Philip that her hopes of a child were false and that he might leave England when he chose. Now that she had surrendered to the inevitable at last he seemed disconcerted and asked embarrassedly, "What will you do while I am away?"

"Sit for Antonio Moro perhaps," replied Mary trying to keep her voice casual. "You would like to have my portrait by you while you are abroad would you not?"

"What need of a portrait when your image is imprinted on my heart," he returned with swift, overdone gallantry.

Mary turned her back on him.

2

On 26 August 1555, through streets crowded with people come in for the Bartholomew Fair, Mary passed through London in a litter with Philip riding on one hand and her cousin, Cardinal Pole, on the other. She was cheered all the way. Her subjects had not laid eyes upon her for so long and there were some who had thought her dead.

The royal party took barge at Tower Wharf for Greenwich Palace. They were received at Greenwich Stairs by Chancellor Gardiner, now a very sick man. His big round eyes were sunk deep in his head and the skin of his face was stretched taut over the blunt nose and high cheekbones.

Three days later Philip left. Mary traversed the galleries of Greenwich Palace with him, loath to let him go. She went as far as the head of the stairs and nearly broke down as he took his leave of her. Then she rushed to a window to watch his barge going down river. She waved to the small, neat figure standing on the after-deck. Philip waved his bonnet at her. Believing herself temporarily alone she gave way to a flood of tears. Sweet Jesu, she prayed, send him back to me soon. Then she reviled herself for her lack of pride. She turned abruptly to see Gomez standing watching her. His face expressed honest pity. She looked at this young, arrogant Spaniard, whom Philip had left behind as a sort of hostage for his return, and to soothe her hurt feelings into believing that he would come back soon. Her hand went up to wipe her streaming eyes and she said slowly, "It would take God Himself to drink this cup." She had the bleak satisfaction of seeing Ruy Gomez start with surprise and drop his eyes.

RICHMOND PALACE

July, 1557

The woman sitting so still before the window in Richmond Palace shut her eyes and shivered as she remembered that first, bitter parting. Of course she had tried to bury herself in work to dull the pain, dealing with every smallest detail of state business, work she could well have delegated to secretaries. She had kept Philip informed of everything discussed by the Privy Council, however trivial, and had sat up far into the night—she could not sleep anyway—writing letters to her husband. She complained to Renard that Philip did not write to her often enough but knew he could do nothing to remedy the matter. She consoled herself by restoring all the old Catholic customs and in 1556 held the ancient Maundy ceremony which had been discontinued in her brother's reign.

Meanwhile the burning of heretics had continued and now that Philip was not by to goad her on she began to doubt the wisdom of burning men for sticking to their opinions, however wrong they might be. The Spaniards started to drift away to Brussels where Philip now was. Ruy Gomez and the remainder of Philip's suite, including his confessor, were sent for. Christmas, 1556 came and went. In January 1557, the Emperor Charles resigned everything to his son save the Empire and Burgundy. Desperately had Mary begged Philip to return to England, hating herself for a humility which should be shown only to God. She had even sent William Paget to Philip to plead on her behalf, so abject a creature had she become. Paget had returned with empty promises. Philip would come at Easter. If not then, at Whitsuntide. But he did not come. Mary raved and cursed, losing her dignity in front of her ladies, and standing before Tiziano Vercelli's portrait of Philip, her knight in shining armour, she raked her nails down that arrogantly smiling face, not caring that she defaced a masterpiece.

And then there had been talk of war. Talk resolved itself into action and Philip had declared war on France. Needing English men and ships he had crossed the Channel in person to ask her for them. He had come to her at Greenwich in

March of this present year and once more she was his humble slave. She was not eager for England to become embroiled in a war with France, but with his facile tongue Philip had persuaded her that it was in England's best interests. The French were plundering English ships he had told her. Henri the Second of France harboured English rebels. He had placed his cool white fingers on her neck and caressed her throat and it had been easy to ignore her empty Exchequer and the fact that Spain alone would reap any benefit to be gained from such a war. When she had agreed to all, her eyes slavishly watching his every gesture, Philip had expressed a desire to go to her chamber that night and had made love to her in the way that she had always dreamed a man should love a woman.

The Queen rose stiffly from her chair. It was time to go to Mass. Her ladies obediently followed her to the chapel. As she sank to her knees before the altar she thought, he stayed two months and now he is gone. Since his going I have missed two periods. Can it be that this time God will answer my prayers after all? Ah, Mary, do not delude yourself yet again. No child stirs in your womb. And yet have I missed. It could be. Oh Jesu, it could be . . .

Epilogue

England went to war with France, allied with Spain, and at first gained some success. Philip captured the French town of St. Quentin and in London *Te Deum* was sung. Quickly, however, the tide turned. The mighty Duc de Guise was put in command of the French armies. It was not long before he and his men had Philip on the run. Victory was a thing of the past for England and Englishmen tasted the bitterness of defeat. Worst of all, Calais and Guisnes, England's sole remaining possessions in France, fell to the French arms and Mary realised too late that she was an Englishwoman. The realisation brought her great sorrow. She had sold herself and England to Spain.

After the fall of Calais and Guisnes in January 1558, Mary lived on for another eleven, illness-plagued months. She was not, of course, pregnant when Philip left England for the second time. She had never been pregnant at any time during her marriage. Her symptoms were born of her intense desire to give Philip a son and England an heir. She died on November 17 1558, a misguided, misunderstood and misused woman, possessing few of the qualities necessary for sovereignty.

At Hatfield a pale, red-haired girl learned that she was to be Queen and with a gesture of defiance threw her rosary out of the window.